BLUE'S PROPHECY

THE CANIS CHRONICLES

EMILY ROSE ROSS
WITH DIANE LORE

To Bill

Please
Enjoy

BLUE'S PROPHECY: THE CANIS CHRONICLES

Library of Congress Cataloging-in-Publication Data on file

For inquiries about volume orders, please contact:

TitleTown Publishing LLC
PO Box 12093
Green Bay WI 54307
Titletownpublishing.com

Published in the United States by TitleTown Publishing
Titletownpublishing.com

Distributed by Midpoint Trade Books
www.midpointtrade.com

Cover Design by Mylène Villeneuve
Interior design by Mark Karis

Printed in the United States of America

For Mom and Dad, who believed in my dreams.

FOREWORD

AS I WRITE THIS, a new generation of athletes is arriving in Brazil for the 2016 Olympics, coming forth from an amazing array of different cultures and talents.

But what they share, whether they're destined for gold, silver, bronze, or obscurity, is a drive to master their sport. During the games, we marvel at the internal fire and punishing training, which—often starting at an early age—has lifted these gymnasts, swimmers, and track stars above the competition. The ability to have laser focus on a goal, even if that means passing on other activities, is not unique to Olympians; it can forecast the winners in fields as different as art and politics, music and business, medicine and literature.

Which brings me to my granddaughter, Emily Ross, who, at age 10, decided to write a novel. A novel about Blue, a scrappy alley dog, and the pack she grows to love.

The family's first clue that Emily had steel in her ambition came from her fourth grade teacher. She was concerned that the introverted little girl in the back row wasn't paying attention to her lessons. And it was all tied to *the book*. A book we knew nothing about. As her mother learned in a parent-teacher conference, Emily was working on it nonstop—"page after page after page, with the daily, dogged determination of Sisyphus. Of course, this was being done during math, social studies, language arts, and even during recess. Okay, this was serious."

Her mother and I, both former journalists, would like to think she has ink in the blood. Or maybe she's been around writing so much, she couldn't imagine not telling her own story.

After all, her ancestry includes a New York editor, a radio columnist, a prize-winning novelist, and a lot of journalists. Even her beloved grandmother—my wife, Rosemary (who most often was resigned to fixing the grammar of everyone else)—finally penned and published her own poetry book after her stroke.

When I moved from Ohio to Atlanta to live with my daughter and her family, I'd often find Emily still up long after the sun had gone down, working on her manuscript on her computer as well as the accompanying drawings and animation. Happily, as time went on, even as her manuscript swelled to over 50,000 words, she made time for her studies and activities such as orchestra (the double bass) and archery, both of which, incidentally, she pursued with almost the same energy as she reserved for *the book*.

We can't know where this early passion for writing will lead, but it's enough for us to know that Emily is capable of bringing dedication, energy, and creativity to any undertaking she chooses to pursue. And, we hope that *Blue's Prophecy* will become a delight and an inspiration for a new generation of young writers and readers.

—DAVID LORE

"The world will not be destroyed by those who do evil, but by those who watch them without doing anything" —ALBERT EINSTEIN

THE DOGS:

ASH: Dingo; sympathetic, altruistic, and skilled, with purple eyes

BALTA: Long-haired Husky who loves snow; bright blue eyes, leader of the snow pack

BLUE: Siberian Husky; bright blue eyes, a hot-headed alley hustler

BLACK TAIL: Black Newfoundland; leader of swamp pack; smart, stubborn, calm, and loyal

BUDDY: German Shepherd; world traveler, crafty and adventurous

CLOVER: Saint Bernard; gentle, German dog who joins Robo's army

COPPER: Bloodhound; resourceful, always tries to do the right thing

DESTINY: Black Lab; smart and timid sister of Max

DUNCAN: Half-wolf; protective and loyal, dark gray except for a white belly

DIAMOND: Siberian Husky with gray; Blue's mom, sly, fierce, protective, and adventurous

JENNY: Chow-chow; leader of desert pack; natural leader, powerful, sometimes nice

KILLER: Pit Bull; Sergeant in Robo's army; strict and manipulative

RAVEN: Great Dane; light gray fur, red eye with white pupil (foretells the future), white eye with red pupil (recounts the past); a wise teacher but lacks patience; loyal to a fault

REX: Coyote; strong; Copper's best friend, Special Forces in SAD army

REY: Chihuahua; a general in SAD army

ROBO: Great Dane with dark gray fur; saved as a puppy by loving family, can be gentle; smart before transformation, genius afterwards; lies, manipulates, and has a lot of charisma; a born leader; robotic eye, ear, and legs

ROVER: Abandoned puppy; half-robot; taken in by the healer, Ash, in Jenny's pack

SABU: Doberman; arrogant, young lieutenant in Robo's army

SAVAGE: German Shepherd; Robo's adopted son and captain of Robo's army

SNIFFER: Beagle; friendly, slick recruiter for Robo's army

SNOW: White wolf; arrogant and beautiful with bright blue eyes

SPLAT: Australian Shepherd; easily intimidated, but loves his pack and is a close friend of Unknown's

UNKNOWN: Mixed breed, most closely resembling a grayhound; meek and shy; very skinny with a gray, crooked nose; the first love of Robo

PART 1

When good twists into bad, and bad grows into good
And flesh and steel become one.

CHAPTER 1

HUMANS. MOST SEEM NICE. But some are just evil.

There were still three who mattered to Robo. And right now they stood next to the stainless steel examining table as the Great Dane lay nearly still, paws twitching. His eyes were heavy and his heart ached. The pain of separation. Again.

He and his family had just reunited, and now here he was in a doctor's sterile office, being ripped away from them, emotionally and physically, once more.

I was such a stupid pup, he thought, slowly closing his eyes as he recalled how he'd lost his family in the first place. Years ago, he had run away from his tidy suburban home, frightened and disoriented by a spring thunderstorm. By the time it stopped, he was lost.

He'd never forgotten his first cold, wet night alone.

But he had also survived against the odds. And within a few short years, he was thriving in the city—rising through hard work and discipline to become a pack leader of a strong, fierce group of stray dogs.

Then, two weeks ago, through chance, his family had found him again—after a lifetime of being separated. He had been at the park, overseeing his pack's patrol, when he suddenly saw Becca, the youngling of the three. He stared at her so long, so overwhelmed by emotion, and she noticed him—no longer a puppy with floppy gray ears, but a massive Great Dane. She peered at him with the same intensity, and then slowly walked toward him. Robo, so sure of himself, so suspicious of humans, found he couldn't move, even when she slowly petted him and checked him for a collar and tags. He didn't even move when she slowly checked his back leg for a telltale heart in his fur, and she gently said, "Oh, Robo. I've missed you so much."

His family immediately encouraged him to join them, calling him to jump into their white minivan. He did. His love for his first pack—his first kind humans—was so powerful, he didn't even consider the magnitude of his decision to leave his dog pack. He was just so happy.

Too happy. He didn't need to worry about survival any more.

On most days, he and Becca explored the lake in their subdivision, with Becca pretending that he was a horse and she was the mighty warrior, looking to save the injured birds that they would sometimes find.

He would watch her at night as she slept. He wouldn't fit in her small mahogany twin bed, but instead, he slept on a thick shag rug next to her, blissfully content.

Honestly, most days were spent chasing squirrels.

And that's how it happened—he had jumped on the deck at a squirrel, only to tumble down the stairs. Robo was hurt badly.

When Becca found him, he could barely move, wheezing in pain. As they loaded him back into the van, his breath became shallow, and he could see fear in Becca's eyes.

And now—they were here. He, on the examining table, Becca draped on his neck, with tears streaming down her check.

Robo had never seen any human as distressed as she was.

He felt her warm tears soak through his fur, and his throat tightened. His eyes began to burn, and he quickly closed them to cool them down. It didn't help. He moved his large head to nuzzle her, and she grasped it in a desperate hug.

"You can't just die!" she whispered into his huge pointed ear. "You just can't." He started to lick her tears. She lifted her hand and scratched behind his ears. Hardly able to move, Robo howled in frustration, his fur standing on end. Becca's mother looked at her, and hugged her.

Robo had always been close to Becca's mom—but like most moms, she hadn't been able to spend the time with him that Becca had. Even so, Robo had always loved sitting under the table near the kitchen island, where her mom, with green eyes and dirty blonde hair, would toss him pieces of cheese when no one was looking.

She also used to take Robo running—less often now than when she was younger. But like Robo, she had strong legs, often covered up by the jeans and cooking aprons she wore daily.

She was a good match with Becca's dad, an alpha whom Robo respected. He had named Robo when he first landed in their home. With black hair, brown eyes, and a broad smile, her dad was a gifted mechanic who had originally named Robo "Robot" for his silky, short gray fur that looked almost metallic in the right light. But Becca couldn't pronounce it, shortening it to Robo, and it stuck.

Robo looked up and realized this was the first time he had ever seen Becca's dad cry.

Suddenly, a door opened, and a man in a white coat walked in with determined long strides, his hands behind his back. Tall with broad shoulders, the doctor had slick black hair and light blue eyes. Robo suddenly realized that he knew this man…and he had unfinished business with him. Mustering all his strength, he snarled and growled at the man. But, strangely, his pack of humans ignored his warnings and walked right to his enemy.

"Is there anything you can do?" Becca said, her voice unsteady. The man stared at the papers attached to his clipboard.

"Trying to act important, aren't you?" Robo growled at the man.

The man ignored him. It was no use. He was a dog, and they were all humans.

The man slowly took off his black-rimmed glasses and sighed.

"I'm sorry, your dog has had a massive heart attack, and I'm not sure I can save him. Just listen—he's growling in pain."

Robo looked at the man. What was he doing? Robo knew—just knew—he had lied.

Mom and Dad both looked at Becca.

"Honey, let's hope for the best," her mother said gently, arms wrapped around Becca.

Becca looked deeply into Robo's eyes, searching for clues. "Robo. Robo, what should I do?" she sobbed. Robo howled from another wave of pain through his chest.

Becca wrapped her arms around him. "Save him," she whispered to the man in the white coat.

Mom and Dad agreed, and slowly patted Becca's back. "Come on, honey, let's go and give the doctor some time."

And with that, each of them—each of his beloved human pack—hugged him around the neck gently, telling him how much they loved him and treasured him. They stroked his fur, and patted his giant head, tears in their eyes.

Then, they were gone.

Robo's heart dropped as he watched his family just leave him there. His chest was burning in pain, and he was having difficulty breathing.

The man turned to him and smirked.

"Robo, I'm not very happy with you. I had great plans for you, and instead, this silly little family got to you first. But now—now that you are mine—our destiny will finally be fulfilled."

Robo growled.

This man—this evil, evil human. This was Dr. Dexter Rune, the man who had murdered his mother.

"Of course, we do have to fix that broken rib," Dexter said lightly. "It was convenient that it happened so near your heart. So easy to tell them that it was a heart attack—a heart attack, I'm afraid, they will believe you did not survive."

He smiled, his white canines looking unnaturally sharp for a human.

Putting his glasses back on, Dexter slowly reached for a syringe that looked just like the one that had killed Robo's mother. Holding it up, Dexter slowly drew liquid in and gently tapped it before plunging it into Robo, who was still strapped down.

"Time to sleep…for now," Dexter said as he slid the syringe in between Robo's shoulders. Robo started to kick and fight as much as he could, but his hearing started to have a strange echo, as if he were underwater, and his vision blurred. His legs stopped moving, and he was weak. He felt his eyelids start to close, and he only had the strength to growl one last time: "I hate you so much."

ঽ⋆

Robo felt sore—very sore. His head was pounding, and he felt dried blood trapped in his fur, on his snout, chest, stomach, and hips. Blood and, strangely, metal, were the only things he could smell. He didn't want to open his eyes. He didn't want to face the outside, and his soreness was quickly turning into searing pain. He just wanted to disappear.

He whimpered, and finally, his pain forced him fully awake. He opened the one eye he could, and saw steel bars. He could open only one of his eyes. He pawed at the other one only to realize there was something on it—*in* it. He started shaking his great head back and forth, rubbing it against the bars, trying to dislodge the thing in his eye. Suddenly, he was leveled by a massive headache. The thing in his eye whirled, giving him full vision along with a stream of numbers and codes scrolling from the left side.

His head dropped in surprise, and the new eye focused on his front right leg, racked in pain. The flesh and fur were gone, replaced with robotic tubes and joints. His back right leg had also been replaced, along with his tail. His beautiful tail that had once wagged in the presence of his human pack was now just interlocking metal rods. He sat down in shock and anger. "What has he done to me?" Robo wailed and barked. He kicked against the cage; he had to get out.

"I can't live like this. *I can't live like this.*"

He howled in despair, tears streaming down the side of his face. Finally, exhausted from the pain and the shock, he gave up, carefully placing his paw over his natural eye.

Hours later, Robo heard the double doors swing open into the laboratory where he was caged. He lifted his head, and his fur stood on end. Three humans, all in white lab coats, entered the room. Two he did not know. The other was Dexter.

Robo looked at Dexter and snarled as viciously as he could. Dexter lifted his arms and shouted to Robo with joy, "Welcome to your new home!" He then laughed as his partners nervously stared at the massive Great Dane with metallic parts.

Robo looked around again at his "home." Steel tables and medical monitors lined the walls, with several cages in the center of the room. Shelves were filled with test tubes, along with samples of hair and blood. Sterile machines beeped, with screens displaying a constant stream of data. There was a security camera in each corner. The room was silent except for the buzz of technology, but he could hear animals through the walls, howling.

Suddenly, his artificial eye displayed, "English. Would you like to start speaking English?" Robo cocked his head and suddenly he felt his throat twist like he was choking—until suddenly he spat out one, simple word: "Why?"

Dexter, upon hearing a dog say his first human word, laughed in triumph. He then shrugged and muttered, "It all has a purpose, Robo, but one simple dog won't understand." He was cut off when Robo howled, "WHY?" so loudly, the entire complex fell silent.

Dexter, still shaking with delight, slowly turned toward

Robo and answered, "Why? Money, my friend. Money. I'm planning to sell you to the military, as if you know what that is. We, or really I, needed something perfect for the prototype and you, Robo, you are perfection," Dexter said. "Smart enough to anticipate any attack, strong enough to survive a nuclear blast."

He sighed deeply. "And, of course, if the military isn't interested, I'm sure there are others who will be. Those not bothered by certain moral aspects of...this." He waved his thin hand toward Robo's robotic legs.

Robo's tears were gone.

Everything is gone, he thought.

Every single thing he loved was either dead, or had inadvertently betrayed him. Every emotion in his body was burned out now. Except one: rage.

And now, as Dexter laughed and shook test tubes, Robo suddenly felt stronger through that rage.

His bloodied legs found their balance, and Robo stood up at his full height—taller and broader than he had been before.

This man was a killer. This man had taken his mom from him. This man brought pain and death to all animals that had the misfortune to encounter him.

"Swept away," he howled, "Gone!"

Suddenly, Robo felt his implanted gears snap into place with a thin metallic barrel telescoping out from his shoulder. The codes in his eye suddenly read "Laser On."

He realized the voice activation had interpreted "gone" as "on."

Robo also realized that he understood *everything*. He understood the lab notes hanging with scotch tape on the walls. He could read the name of the cage manufacturer that had built his jail, as well as the names of his captors, spelled out carefully on badges clipped to their coats. Dexter, of course, but also John Fox and William Lena.

John Fox was short and timid. William Lena was extraordinarily tall, with hair combed back tightly against his scalp. Robo also got an instinctual whiff that William didn't want to be here either. He looked nervous, and whenever he looked at Dexter, a strange blaze of dislike flashed in his eyes.

But what interested Robo the most were the lines of codes and numbers reeling past in his electronic eye. He now knew what they meant—and what he could do.

Quickly, he muttered, "Activate."

The laser turned on and instantly cut through Robo's cage door. He slammed his shoulder against the broken links and jumped to the floor, sliding briefly on the tile.

Dexter stopped laughing.

"Engage," Robo commanded, with weaponry firing from his shoulder at his will—destroying monitors, test tubes, and shelving, which burst into flames. The men's surprise quickly turned to panic.

Robo, flexing his new body and power, continued to cause chaos, turning his attention toward each piece of medical equipment and setting it ablaze.

All three men scuffled toward the double doors—the only exit. John and William got out, but Dexter, the one Robo wanted, was shoved aside, pushed into a corner as the flames and smoke engulfed the room.

Robo jumped easily over the rising flames, the heat barely

bothering him. He slowly crouched down and started stalking Dexter. Only the red glow of his mechanical eye was visible in the smoke, glaring unblinkingly at Dexter.

"Robo, I'm not the only one who knows about you," Dexter yelled. "They will find you and destroy you."

He then looked in horror at the half-dog, half-machine walking toward him. Dexter started to curl up in the corner, caught between flames and a growing tangle of live wires dangling and sparking from melted machinery.

Robo closed his eyes for a brief second. He saw a vision of Becca, his most beloved human. "I love you, Robo," she said. "Always."

His eyes opened. His rage—and a new, strange strength—pulsed through him.

Dexter stared on in disbelief, barely comprehending the huge beast illuminated by the flames around him.

"What have I created?" he whispered, shrinking back.

"You—you are a murderer," Robo said slowly. "You have created a new beginning."

Robo looked Dr. Dexter Rune one last time before leaving him to his fate, and leapt through the doors and into the night.

He did not even pause when he heard the explosion.

CHAPTER 2

FROM THE BEGINNING, Dr. Dexter Rune had ruined every-thing in Robo's life.

He had first met Dexter at the puppy mill where he had been born. Puppy mills were very different from stores with adorable, well-cared-for puppies. Here, in run-down barns, mother dogs were kept in small pens, forced to turn out litter after litter of pups until they died of exhaustion.

For Robo's mom, a gentle Great Dane with a majestic grace, life was particularly hard. She was sleek but large, even for her breed, making the pen even more cramped, and caring for her puppies more difficult. Over the years, her silky fur gave way to scabs. She tried the best she could to shield Robo from the realities of her life, but even she couldn't hide the pain after Dexter arrived.

"I want that one," he said, pointing to her. The puppy mill owner opened the pen, and loomed over her as she crouched in the back, hiding Robo behind her. "Come here, girl," he said in a sing-song voice that even Robo knew not to trust. His mother wouldn't budge, and finally the owner yanked her by the legs and dragged her out of the pen, leaving Robo shivering uncontrollably. Every night she would return with some new wound, and refused to talk to Robo about anything that hap-pened for those long hours.

This went on for weeks, until one night they rolled his

mother into the pen, bleeding and barely conscious. He immediately licked her head and whimpered.

"My darling," she whispered. "Escape from here if you get a
chance, by any means possible. Never let him get his hands on
you." She wheezed in pain. "Baby, I love you so much. I'm so
sorry that I can't save you myself."

That night, Robo snuggled under her muzzle, and she kept
him warm with her great gray paws surrounding him.

By morning, she was cold. The puppy mill owner threw her
body in a dumpster.

The next day, Becca's family showed up at the mill. Of
course, they weren't let into the dirty pens in the back. Instead
the owner loaded all the puppies he could grab into a wheel-
barrow and dumped them into a play yard, surrounded by a
pretty white picket fence and flowers in baskets.

The other puppies, hungry and infested with fleas, could
barely move. But Robo, remembering what his mother said,
mustered up his last bit of strength to nuzzle the young girl and
her parents. He was lively, nipped at her heels, and played with
the red ball she gently rolled to him.

"Oh, you are just so cute," Becca said, rubbing his soft gray
ears. "I just want to love on you non-stop." Her parents laughed,
and pulled out a credit card to pay for Robo. Becca slipped a
brand new pink collar on him and whispered to him, "I'm sorry,
I really thought I was going to get a girl."

She carried Robo in the crook of her arm as they got into
the mini van. It wasn't until he looked through the window that
he saw Dexter screaming at the owner.

Though he was only a puppy, he knew he had won. Looking

at the dust rising from the back of the car as they drove out of the farm, he made a vow: "Mom, I promise you, he'll pay."

Robo then fell asleep in the safety of his human pack's embrace.

But the seed of rage was planted.

❧

Life with Becca was wonderful. The love was intoxicating, making the pain of his mother's death bearable. He was adored by all and treated as a member of the family. Even when he had nightmares about the puppy mill, Becca pulled him close while he howled in grief in his sleep.

Becca worked with him all summer, teaching him discipline and good manners. He eagerly learned, happy to make her happy, happy to be in good standing with his family. They did everything together—there were McDonald's ice cream cones and dog biscuits, campfires, and swims in the ocean.

The anxiety, however, never really went away. Robo would sometimes marvel at the fact that he had been snatched from death and placed into the arms of those who loved him. It didn't seem fair to all the dogs he had watched die, and he didn't believe he was special enough to have survived.

That anxiety ended up being his undoing. He was always nervous when there were thunderstorms, hiding under the huge dining room table. Sometimes Becca would join him, pulling him into her lap and talking to him in her most soothing tones. But the fear was still there. The storms seemed so powerful, and he seemed so small in comparison. They all seemed small.

One night, there was a particularly bad spring storm. There

were threats of tornadoes, and the family huddled in the stair-well, the radio blaring weather updates and the parents checking their cell phones.

He was terrified.

Then there was a crack of lightning and the door in the stairwell blew open. Robo bolted, slipping out of the collar that Becca desperately tried to hold onto in the dark.

He was blinded by fear and anxiety. The rain pelted him in the face. He ran over the broken branches, dodged the head-lights of cars, and could not stop until the next morning, when he collapsed from exhaustion.

He was lost.

Becca and her family put up posters, and checked shelters. Every night, her mother stroked her hair, while Becca cried and clutched Robo's leather collar. Her father tried to tell Becca that none of this was her fault—that sometimes, things just happen. But Becca didn't believe him. She couldn't believe him. Instead, she vowed before going to bed each night: "Robo, I promise, I'll find you."

But for now, all she could do was wait. Because sometimes, what a girl wants and what life gives her are two different things.

꙰

Robo didn't last a day away from home before he was captured, along with another gray dog called Unknown. She was as young as he was, and had deep scars covering her body. They were forced into a cage inside of a hot van, which drove for hours before stopping.

The cages were taken from the van and brought inside a mountain—a mountain that seemed to hide horrible secrets.

Robo felt alone and scared, and he no longer had a human to help him through his nightmares.

Unknown was in the cage next to him, and would give him comfort—talking in low tones and telling him to not give up, to never abandon hope. He was meant to be something amazing, and they both had to live.

He believed her. And he grew to love her.

Then, Robo saw him.

Dr. Dexter Rune.

This time, Dexter was arguing with a woman who pointed at Robo. Robo didn't understand, but he knew it was bad. He was then moved into a small room with only a desk and empty cages. Dexter, having recognized Robo from his heart birthmark, mumbled, "It's about time."

Then, for months, Dexter ran tests on Robo, injecting him with needles, and shocking him with electric pulses.

He clipped Robo's ears to a sharp point, causing them to bleed for hours. No more did Robo have his "pretty floppy ears" that Becca would gently flip back and forth as she read.

Soon, Robo's gray fur started to fall out from stress, and his only good moments were in his sleep, dreaming of Becca curled up with him.

One day, Robo woke to the sound of sirens. Humans in blue suits were swarming through the mountain's laboratories, followed by people in black uniforms, armed with assault rifles. A woman in a lab coat ran over to his cage, unlocked it, and snatched Robo. She muttered something angrily as she started to run, but was cut off by a uniformed officer who yelled, "Stop"—a word he knew well. The women dropped Robo without any consideration, and tried to keep running, but the man tackled her, and handcuffed her hands behind her back.

Again, Robo saw his chance to survive. He scrambled to his feet and ran through the halls, trying to find any route to the exit. But it was all filled with smoke and chaos. He couldn't see much—the only lights were the dim emergency lights in the halls. There were dogs everywhere, barking, whimpering and running. That's when Robo found Unknown standing in the center of the chaos, her ears torn and her ribs showing. Her eyes landed on Robo, and both were happy to find each other.

They escaped together through a huge steel door, which was left open in the side of the mountain.

Unknown took him back to her pack in the city, which was led by a leader named Bone. Robo, who still mourned the loss of his mother, and now his human family, was not accepted instantly. But after consistently bringing back food and, with his huge size, protecting the smaller dogs and puppies, the pack accepted him—and then, respected him.

As he aged, he became wiser. Soon, he became the leader of Unknown's pack. Bone was chased off, after breaking the pack rules by falling in love with an outsider stray. After announcing that true love was more important than pack loyalty, Bone left—and Robo took his place. Robo took it seriously, caring for the pack with the same dedication he had learned from Becca and her family.

But while he was patrolling his territory, he saw Becca. And Becca found him. And his heart skipped a beat.

Surely this is a sign, he thought. *Surely going back to Becca was meant to be. Surely this is my destiny.*

And in a way, he was right.

CHAPTER 3

BLUE PANTED FOR BREATH, her long white fur raised and anger pulsing though her. "Get back here, you furball!" She ran after him. He had stolen her food, and she wasn't going to let him get out of this city. The brown, small dog took a sharp right down into an ally, and Blue easily followed.

This dog, a feisty terrier, might be small and flexible, but Blue could tell from a lack of scars that he hadn't lived in the back alleys of Atlanta for long.

He didn't seem to know he was running straight into a dead end. Blue gained on him, and quickly snapped onto his tail. He yelped in pain, and he swerved around, his eyes wide. Blue towered over him as he quickly backed away from her.

"Pl-please," he stuttered. Blue twitched her ear. "I just need to head home."

Blue burst into laughter. "Then what was that stunt you pulled with my food?" she snarled. "By the way, where is my food?" The dog studied his paws, his eyes turning watery.

"I-I ate it."

Blue curled her lips. Her blue eyes pierced deeply into his brown ones.

"You what? I'm sorry, I must not have heard you," she said sarcastically.

He attempted to slowly back away from her, but she followed, her paw finally pinning him down.

"Pl-please I just need to get back to my family, They left me at the park and I need to fi-"

Blue cut him off, laughing a deep, cold, scary laugh. "Your family abandoned you, stupid mutt."

He eyes widened, and he shook his head. "That can't be. They love me!"

Blue snickered. "Whatever you say." She turned around and began to walk away.

"I'll let you slide with this one, mutt. It's a gift from this fair city."

But then she turned her head to look at him one last time and growled. "But if I find you stealing my food again, you will be...you know..."

Blue quickly trotted down the gravel path, following the railroad. She was heading home.

Suddenly, a piercing siren rang in her ears. An ambulance. She quickly turned her head toward the noise.

"What the heck?" Blue momentarily felt curious about what was going on, but felt it pass on just as quickly. After all, there were always sounds in the city: ambulances, police cars, fire trucks, cars honking, and people talking. She was used to all of it—and she didn't really care that much about humans, or even dogs for that matter, as long as they didn't bother her. As a matter of fact, if she really thought about it, there was only one person she cared about. Well, not technically cared about— more like loathed.

The dogcatcher. Also known as the dark ghost. Also known as Harold. She snorted just thinking about him.

Oddly, she heard some laughter nearby. It seemed out of

place, considering the recent wail of the ambulance.

But there, on the sidewalk, two girls were on a bench, holding hot dogs and giggling. Stupid kids.

Her stomach growled, and she licked her lips. Turns out she was going to eat today. Blue decided to use a technique she had learned from her mother.

ॐ

Her mother. Diamond. Blue sighed gently.

Blue had not seen her for two years. A husky with long, soft fur and light blue eyes, her mother was able to move silently and carefully through the human world. Other dogs had nicknamed her Silent Paws for her stealth and cunning, and her ability to survive with a puppy in the hustle and bustle of streets and sky-scrapers without a mate. It took work. Diamond was often tired at the end of the day when they would settle into their makeshift den in an abandoned old trash container, hidden in the alley behind a coffee shop. On some nights, her eyes became bright, and she would tell great stories, sharing her adventures around the world with Blue. But most nights, Blue would simply curl into her side, and her mom would wrap her feathery white tail around her. They would fall asleep exhausted, surrounded by the earthy scent of warm fur and coffee.

To others, Blue's mom was a loner—distrustful and quiet. But with her daughter, she was affectionate and playful, bringing home potatoes for them to bat around, chase, and chew. One time, she could barely keep her eyes open from fatigue, yet she still played potato games for hours just to make Blue happy. Sometimes, when Diamond was too tired to run or wrestle, she used a scrap of mirror to cast a spot of reflected sunlight around the alley for Blue to chase.

But when Blue became older, they started arguing more. Blue was hungry, as always, and Diamond was too tired to forage for food. She had been getting thinner and more tired, giving what little food she could gather to Blue.

On this day, she could barely walk.

Blue was resentful. Why didn't she have a stronger mother? Why didn't she have a father who could help? Why were they living in an alley, in an abandoned trashcan? She knew other dogs had it better—she saw them all over the city, sitting in purses or walking with their humans slowly because they were so fat from food she didn't have.

Diamond felt guilty, but was also irritated that her daughter couldn't be more understanding. "You're spoiled," Diamond barked at her. "You don't know how bad things can be."

Blue turned away in anger. "We're eating rats. How much worse can it be?" she whined. "Why can't you understand? Why can't you just leave me alone?!" before running out of the alley.

That evening, she got her wish.

Blue slowly made her way back home, thinking about the best way to apologize. As she arrived, she saw some people in the coffee shop talking gently to her mom. They lured her mom closer with promises of scraps and leftovers of ham and egg sandwiches—food that Diamond surely thought she could bring back and feed to her hungry daughter.

In horror, Blue saw them snatch her mother and carry her inside the shop. Diamond protested, twisting her head around and barking for Blue, not knowing she was there. She became exhausted quickly and she could no longer fight. Blue, suspicious of the humans, hid.

For days, Blue would visit the shop secretly. She kept hoping to see a glimpse of her mom, but after a few weeks, she gave up. Her mom, she feared, was gone. And finally, howling at night in grief and guilt, she left.

❧

Blue's stomach growled again.

She needed food, and it was time to use a technique her mother taught her: "Rabies."

Blue sprang in front of the girls, growling, and staring steadily into their eyes with feigned hatred. She spat foam from her mouth, making her look sick, fearsome, and deadly.

The girls immediately yelled in fear and ran, dropping their hot dogs before fleeing. Blue carefully picked up the two hot dogs and walked to the back of the alley.

She had only taken one bite before she heard, "Aren't you going to share that...Blue?" She lifted her head slowly with annoyance, and saw two huge Rottweilers, the bullies of the alley.

"With what? Your slobbery mouths?" she said, trying to figure out how to save her dinner.

The dogs ignored the comment, instead stepping closer toward the hot dogs. The slightly larger dog growled, "You're going to give us those hot dogs."

Blue slowly looked up and said, "I have no choice."

For a moment, they looked shocked at her decision. But before they had a chance to pick up the hot dogs, she sprang up onto a box, and from there to a big green dumpster, and then the roof. She only peeked back to see how quickly they were gaining on her. "Oh, how the tables have turned on me," she muttered. She was almost home free with only one more leap between two buildings separating her from enjoying her dinner—and victory—in peace.

She jumped and for a moment it seemed that she had cleared the gap. Instead, she missed it, and fell into a trough of water that broke her fall, but then tipped her, wet and cold, onto the concrete.

She looked at her hot dogs. They were now soggy, and gnats had already started circling. It wouldn't stop the Rottweilers from eating them, but they were just rotten now like everything in the city. The Rottweilers set upon the hot dogs—and then, Blue. When they were done, she limped down the sidewalk toward home, beaten, bruised, and still hungry.

That is when she felt the thick cable against her neck, a loop that tightened every time she pulled against it. She spun around in rage and frustration, twisting and turning to try and break the cable. But the loop was attached to a long metal pole, and the man controlling it would not let go.

She recognized him. "Harold," she snarled.

He slid the cable tighter, but then suddenly paused—maybe from fatigue?

Blue tried to take advantage of the moment, jerking the rod as hard as she could to try and break it from his hands. But Harold recovered, shaking his head. He pulled the cord so tight, Blue lost consciousness.

The last words she heard were his: "You're mine now, mutt."

CHAPTER 4

ROBO LIMPED THROUGH THE STREETS, each step agonizing.

His robotic ear could pick up and distinguish among all the city's distinct sounds that made up the loud hum of too much traffic and too many people. It made his other ear seem deaf. People quickly scrambled away from him, their eyes widening and their hands clasped over their mouths. Robo glared at them as he walked by, stiffly, dried blood still clotted in his short fur.

His robotic back leg lifted high every time it moved. Robo snarled low and menacingly toward those who came too close, and he looked straight ahead.

Robo knew this city. He had first learned the pampered side when he loved a family, filled with dog beds, homemade treats, and silly Halloween costumes. Then he had learned the city's heartless side—the dirty streets and the coldness toward an overgrown puppy who had lost his way in a thunderstorm. This side he remembered precisely—the dilapidated buildings, broken businesses, cruel people, and abandoned dogs.

As he turned a corner, he came face-to-face with a man towering over a Husky that was restrained around the neck by a wire linked into a metal pole.

The Husky growled with frustration as the man dragged her. She snarled and yanked at the cable, her fur bristling, before he finally tightened its loop around her throat. Robo growled, not so much in sympathy with the Husky—dogs like this were a dime a dozen—but because he hated dog catchers. Loathed them.

The man was struggling to hold on to his metal pole, the Husky still yanking him from side to side. He suddenly jerked backwards and stared directly at Robo.

His eyes widened in terror—and momentary intrigue. "You're next," he muttered under his breath, before pulling the wire so hard, the Husky passed out. He leaned down and whispered to her before loading her into his truck.

Robo narrowed his eyes, carefully memorizing the man's fat face and beady eyes, before returning to his journey.

After several blocks, Robo turned into the alley he recognized: pawn shop on the right, BBQ chicken joint on the left. Bounding down the dark narrow passage, damp with rain and heat, he easily leaped over dumpsters and crates.

Finally, Robo reached a small, abandoned building.

Its roof had collapsed, and there were no more windows left for the teens to smash. He smelled the air, sniffing for familiarity, for signs.

It had been months since he had been to this place, since he lived with Becca, before he was tortured by Dexter.

He smelled mud, and found a broken hose dripping into a large, clear puddle outside the rundown building. Robo saw his reflection for the first time since his transformation. He momentarily felt his chest tighten with grief. Once he had been a beautiful Great Dane, with soft gray hair and clear, bright eyes. Two eyes.

It seemed that half of his head was now metal. What wasn't metal was scarred, reflecting a tough life in the streets.

He sighed, dipped his natural paw in the water, and raised

it up to wash the blood off his head and legs. A little cleaner, Robo then realized the metal now concealed one of the most important scars he had ever received.

Robo remembered the utter pain he was in when another dog had slashed his claws across Robo's right eye. Dr. Dexter Rune had blocked most of the scar with the new robotic eye, as well as placing metal implants where there had once been a torn ear and a deeply gashed back leg.

But Robo didn't want those scars to be concealed. Every scar he carried was a reminder of survival and vengeance.

The scar on his eye—the nastiest one—had been caused by Unknown, who had grown up to be a gray, skinny, mixed breed with a crooked snout. Robo still loved her. He didn't really understand why he did—she wasn't pretty or even that smart. The things they had endured together as puppies caused him to love her—enough to fight a battle for her. After all that, he still had to watch Unknown choose someone else. A half-wolf named Colin had stolen the only dog beside his mother that Robo had loved.

Robo snapped out of the memory. He sighed and looked a final time at his reflection. A smile started to creep over his jaw, revealing perfect, metallic canine teeth. He walked deeper into the allyway, his claws scraping through rocks and dust, to a smaller, darker passageway. Robo felt his fur touch both sides of the walls. As he walked down the path, he thought about Savage, an adorable little pup he'd saved from the previous pack leader.

Now you're lying to yourself, too, he thought ruefully, remembering all the times he'd lied to Savage to keep the puppy in check.

It had worked. Now Savage was his Beta, and more importantly, his strongest ally.

Robo looked up and was startled by a bright light in front of him. He walked quicker, his heart pumping with hope that his pack was still there. He was the Alpha, after all.

He finally entered the abandoned tower he knew, a sky-scraper torn apart by age and poverty. A light in the once great hall blinded him for a second, but as he opened his eyes, he could see hundreds of dogs on the broken concrete floors, sleeping, eating, or taking care of pups.

He looked at the pile of concrete blocks in the center of the building. Savage sat on top of them. He had dark circles under his eyes, which were deep set and mysterious—this is how he always looked. With his snout in the air, Savage surveyed the area, making sure everyone was doing everything right.

Savage's gaze landed on Robo, and his eyes widened. Savage leaped forward and landed squarely in front of the Great Dane.

"Robo's back! Robo's back!" Savage howled. The pack members turned quickly and stared at the two.

A silence filled the hall, making Robo's robotic ear strain for sound.

"What happened to you?" Savage said, quickly backing away from Robo, stunned.

"Humans did this to me," Robo whispered just loud enough for Savage to hear.

Savage looked around at all the dogs there, fur bristling with horror. "Did I stutter?" he snarled. "I said our Alpha has returned!"

The dogs exchanged glances with each other before giving false smiles. Robo had left them for a human.

Robo scanned the pack for friendly faces until he found

Unknown, sitting in the corner, her yellow-green eyes emotionless.

Unknown noticed Robo looking at her. She circled tightly, lying down to face the wall.

Robo shook his head in disgust. It's a good thing he had stopped loving her a long time ago. Yet he still couldn't shake a small twinge of hurt.

Robo turned back to Savage, who smiled with true pleasure.

"Follow me!" Savage barked with enthusiasm, and bounded toward some black ladders that the dogs hadn't been able to get up in the past. "We figured out how to get onto the roof," Savage said as he pushed a long wooden board that leaned on a wall onto a ladder, making it into a ramp. He scrambled to the roof, and Robo easily followed. They could see the city from up here.

"So, now that you're back home, what are you going to do? Do you want to rest, or do want to make the pack bigger or…" Savage was cut off when Robo lifted his paw in the air.

"Savage, there's a bigger plan now," Robo said. "Things are changing. Humans are getting worse—just look at what they did to me. I think we need to find a place that is safer, somewhere where our pups can play without the threat of dogcatchers, without being hit by cars, without hunger."

Robo took a deep breath.

"I know a better place—Unknown knows it too—but it means the pack will have to make a big journey. The pack will have to trust me." Robo nodded to Savage. "The good news is, I can see they already trust you."

Savage bowed slightly at the compliment. "The pack will follow me—and you," he said. "Tell me more about where we will be living?"

Robo leaned closer to Savage. "We're going to live in a mountain.

"*In* a mountain?" Savage said, looking confused.

"Yes, *in* a mountain," Robo said quietly. "Tell the pack to prepare."

CHAPTER 5

STAINLESS STEEL MESH SURROUNDED BLUE. She looked around at the cage, which had barely enough room for her to stand and turn around. She was disoriented, and didn't know where she was. Dogs barked in rage. Blue was terrified. Her back hurt. She tried to sit up, to stretch a little, but she hit her head against the sheet steel ceiling. She was cramped. They were all cramped.

And they were all trying to break out.

Within hours, she, too, was slamming against the door. After that terrible decision, Blue's head and shoulders were bruised, and she was worn out. Blue growled, before circling into a ball for sleep.

She already missed her alley behind the coffee shop. *Ah, nothing like home—infested with maggots, and killer dogs. And a missing mother*, she thought cynically. Blue closed her eyes, but she couldn't sleep. "I'll just rest for a moment," she muttered. But as the hours wore on, exhaustion crept over her, and sleep finally arrived.

Suddenly, a human voice broke through the dogs' barking.

"Becca, please be quick about this. We don't have much time." A woman with blonde hair looked impatiently at a teenager with long brown hair.

The girl walked briskly from cage to cage. Blue quickly leaned against the back of her cage, praying not to be seen.

It didn't work. The girl stood directly in front of her. Blue didn't know how to play this. Whimper? Snarl? What would her mother do?

The girl didn't seem to care how she acted. Instead she whispered quickly to Blue, "Hi! I'm Becca."

The conversation quickly ended when her mother snapped, "Don't even think about that one. She's a Husky—too much energy, too wild."

Becca frowned and looked wistfully at Blue before standing up and walking away. Blue suddenly felt sad. She didn't even know why. Minutes later, a new person stopped at her cage. He was very tall, well groomed, and carried an expensive leather briefcase. Harold gleefully walked next to him, trying to catch up to his long strides.

"I need a strong, energetic, smart dog," the tall man said in a deep, confident voice.

Harold nodded, glaring at Blue as they walked past her. Blue rolled her eyes and turned her attention back towards the cage.

As the men walked around the corner, Blue reexamined the lock. She stared at the wire "S" latch, and realized that her snout would work as well as a human's finger to lift the lock. Testing the theory, she scraped her nose against the metal. The first time it didn't work, snagging halfway through. After a few more tries, she felt the latch lift. The cage door swung open, and she quietly took a step out.

"Hey!"

Blue turned around to see Harold running toward her. *This is getting old*, she thought with annoyance. She tried "Rabies" with the foam forming around her mouth—but Harold didn't flinch. "You think I haven't picked up on your stupid tricks?" he yelled as he moved forward.

Blue tried to run away, but was slammed to the ground, the wire stick too quick for her. She shook her head, trying to loosen Harold's grip on the wire.

Finally, Blue managed to twist enough to bite the stick and rip it out of Harold's hands. The twist was so violent that the stick whirled around and smacked Harold in the face. Blue let out a small yelp of delight. "Ha! You idiot!"

Harold groaned, looking at Blue. He shakily got up and spat out blood. "You stupid, no-good mutt!"

The tall man stepped in between Harold and Blue.

"I'll take her."

They both looked at the tall man. Blue tried to run away, but Harold grabbed the stick dragging on the ground, the loop still around her neck, and pulled her back to his side. "Oh, of course!"

The tall man nodded. "Great."

Harold sneered. "Great."

Blue let out a sigh. "Great."

CHAPTER 6

ROBO QUICKLY REGAINED CONTROL of his pack with his sharp barks and robotic power. His first command was for them to make preparations to leave in exactly one moon cycle.

The dogs, comfortable under the less harsh rule of Savage, had at first hesitated when Robo told them to get ready to move out. But they knew that Robo had always watched out for them, keeping them safe from a world that killed strays without thinking.

Robo perceived the initial reaction, not understanding why the pack seemed so scared of his presence. But the Alpha knew how to be a leader. He softened his tone. Robo started to reunite with some of the bolder and older members, while gently nudging and playing with the scared—but curious—pups that had arrived in the months since he had left.

When the time was right, he moved to the front of the pack. Savage followed a couple footsteps behind him. Slowly, the hundreds of dogs, mutts and purebreds, large and small, started falling in behind the two leaders.

Robo winced for a second. He was still in pain from Dexter's surgeries, but he knew he had felt worse.

Robo led his pack out of the broken-down building. He turned around to see Splat, an Australian shepherd. Fur covered Splat's eyes, and he walked silently—and uncomfortably—next to Unknown.

"Why is he still upset?" Robo muttered under his breath. A year ago, Robo had given him a chance to be part of his pack. But Splat never really spoke when Robo was around. Robo had seen him happy and playing with the other dogs, but with one glance at Robo, he would turn quiet or slowly retreat in the dens.

Ungrateful, Robo thought, irritated. *All of them.*

In small groups, the pack turned around to say goodbye to their home and its memories, and then left it behind, running with Robo into the street.

The humans were stunned, watching hundreds of dogs stream toward them, teeth bared. Robo observed the humans—so far removed from their primal selves. Most watched in fascination, some pulling out their cell phones to record the dogs, instead of being afraid.

They are soft, he thought with contempt.

Even the younglings had no sense of danger. One toddler, amazed at all the dogs, yelled "Puppies" and started to waddle toward Robo, her hands outstretched. Savage nervously looked at her and then at Robo and back at her.

Robo stood still. For a brief second, he saw Becca—his Becca. But he regained focus. When the little girl was close enough, he growled a warning, and nipped her hand—softly, but hard enough to push her to the ground.

She looked at him, wounded and surprised, as she lay on the ground, her eyes filling with tears. "Baddy! Baddy!" she wailed.

Robo's robotic ear started ringing from the sound, and any tenderness he felt evaporated. "Shut up already," he growled, before feeling a sharp pain hit him in the side. He snarled, and looked up at the youngling's mother, her nose flaring with rage.

Her lips were curled, and he saw her form a fist, smacking Robo as quick as lightning. He yelped in surprise, and jumped away from her. She followed him, giving a hard kick in his robotic leg. He jumped away again, shocked. He respected this mother—viciously protecting her pup. But he had barely touched the youngling; he had just tried to get her to stop screaming.

Humans. Always either overreacting or oblivious.

Robo looked back at Savage, and twitched his ear to signal him to go. Savage nodded, before yelling, "Come on!" to the pack, and continued charging through the streets. Robo winked his approval to his Beta, and followed. As the night fell, Robo and Savage led the pack through back roads, through the northern suburbs of Atlanta, and later, the pine forests of the Piedmont of rural Georgia. They let the moonlight guide them toward the single mountain, a great, black, jagged, edge against the dark blue sky.

"If we don't stop, we'll make it by sunrise," Robo called out to his pack. "We'll rest in the morning."

The dogs barked their agreement.

The march continued.

❧

Hours later, Robo and Savage were deep in their own thoughts, when suddenly Robo saw a flash of white through the pine trees. He turned quickly to try and capture the movement.

"Robo?" Savage asked.

Robo, nose in the air, looked at Savage. "Go without me. I'll catch up later."

Savage stared at him for a couple of seconds and nodded.

Robo slowly followed the scent of dog... and humans? Robo shook his head. There's no way humans would be in this part of the woods at this time of night.

Then he saw her, moving alarmingly fast. His robotic eye caught an infrared vision of the same husky once struggling in the street. She had escaped!

Robo's eyes widened and he swallowed hard. *What are they doing out here?* he thought, crouching in the tall grass.

He tried to get a better lock on her, but she was already gone, slipping through the high grass and into the cover of darkness.

"Don't worry, Husky. I'll save you." Robo felt his heart harden a little more toward humans. No more Becca. No more family. No more mercy.

He had seen so many things happen to dogs when they had done nothing to the humans except be their loyal—*too* loyal—companions.

Robo dug his claws deep into the earth. They needed to be punished. Not just the scientists, not just the mother who hit and kicked him, not just the dogcatcher—all of them.

But how, he thought. *How?*

His mind, initially foggy from Dexter's operations, now recalled the image of a shining, bright blue, fiery ball. He had first seen it through the bars of his cage. He remembered watching it be used to destroy everything—concrete, bricks, steel, drones, tanks...and dogs. A beam of light, and then nothing—everything reduced to dust. As it glowed and rotated slowly in its case, the scientists had stepped back to congratulated each other, slapping each other on the back. Robo recognized this happiness, this self-important moment, even without understanding exactly what they were saying.

Robo realized now that he and the orb were intended to be the ultimate pairing of weapons. A dog that could destroy targets precisely, like a surgeon's blade, backed up by an orb that could destroy everything left, like a shotgun blast.

No longer would humans need coal, oil, or nuclear fission for energy. This—this glowing ball—could power anything, and still fit in a man's pocket. Robo closed his eyes. He would find it and use it to destroy the very human race that built it.

But...

Had it survived the fire?

Robo was determined to find out. If it did, he—with the help of his pack and those two surviving scientists—would be able to beat the humans at their own violent game.

Humans would return to being the naked, soft creatures they had been. After centuries of ruling the animals, they would not be prepared for the animals *to fight back.*

His lips curled at the thought, revealing his metallic teeth in the moonlight.

CHAPTER 7

FAR FROM THE CAGES AT THE SHELTER, this new place was deep in the woods. The tall man unloaded Blue from the truck parked next to a large tree that, from the smell, or lack of smell, wasn't a tree at all. It was sterile: no whiffs of animals, birds, bugs, or even wood. Tall Man leaned into the hooded lens of a security camera, which did a quick retinal scan, before the hidden doors opened to a steep staircase down into the ground.

Workers in spotless white suits quickly surrounded Blue and, despite her growling and snapping at them, talked gently before injecting her. Scared and confused, she became aware of wires, test tubes, and the smell of her own blood.

"How's it going?" one scientist said to the other.

"She's doing very well, despite the high charges we've been giving her," said the other.

Blue snarled.

"Don't worry, girl," the first scientist said. "This only hurts a little bit." He stabbed her with another needle.

Suddenly, strangely, she felt stronger. But as she looked at her reflection into the shiny, stainless steel table, she was struck by a far bigger difference. Her blue eyes were now bright— almost glowing.

Blue had been named such by her mother because of her almost instant love affair with water. As a puppy, Blue would boldly bound through puddles during thunderstorms, and even as an adult, she would paddle in the city ponds when the police weren't watching.

But this was different. Blue, like most Huskies, already had pale blue eyes. Only now they were a piercing aqua, the color of the sea and the sky—a color so intense, there was nothing natural about it.

"What the heck?" Blue snarled. "Get me out of here!"

She clawed to get off of the table, but couldn't get traction, her paws uselessly scraping back and forth against the polished steel. The scientists again rushed to the table, locking a collar around her neck, two of them keeping her from thrashing her head from side to side.

They dragged her outside, despite her angry barks.

And then, they unlocked the collar.

Freedom!

Blue sprinted from her captors—a far easier and faster journey than she thought possible. She ran through the forest, her nose leading past the trees, grass, and creeks. Within a day, she was back among the garbage cans, sidewalks, cardboard shelters, the homeless, the noise, and chaos.

It was good to be home.

❧

Within a few days, her old friend, hunger, was back.

She searched through a trashcan and picked up a moldy, half-eaten sandwich. "Score!" Blue yipped before chewing on it with gusto.

After finishing, the hunger pains delayed for a few hours, she turned around toward the street. There, in the middle of the street, she noticed a rusty cage, and whimpering sounds of puppies. Blue cocked her head in confusion.

Then Blue saw her old friends, the Rottweiler bullies. As they walked toward the cage, laughing, she realized they planned to kill the pups. They had a long history of terrorizing—murdering cats, squirrels, or any other defenseless animals unfortunate enough to cross their path when they were bored.

Blue muttered to herself as she bounded into the street to get the cage, "Not today."

She knew something was different within her. She still didn't know how to control her new power, but somehow she was going to move that cage.

Within seconds, she had easily beaten them to the cage. *I've got this*, she thought.

She snarled at them, "You're not killing these puppies."

She then grabbed the cage bars in her mouth to drag it off the street. Only one problem—she couldn't move it.

"Crap."

Apparently, she did not "got this." She wasn't different. She had no special powers, and no special strength.

The Rottweilers, who had moved back in surprise after she rushed in, were laughing on the sidewalk.

As she stared remorsefully back at the cage, she saw a speeding car headed right for her.

Clearly, the driver only saw the rusty cage, and, with rush hour traffic on both sides, decided to hit it, and Blue, too.

With the puppies' yelps of terror, she could feel her own adrenalin surge. She decided to perform one last, noble act, stepping in front of the cage in an attempt to shield them. Blue prayed for forgiveness for all that she had done wrong in her short life. She looked inside the cage and said, "I can't save you."

The car hit her broadside. She felt the force of the impact, heard the screeching of brakes, and smelled rubber from the tires. But she could still feel the street under her paws.

Am I dead? she thought, confused. *Where's the white light? The Open Meadow?*

She opened her eyes. People encircled her, swarming the sidewalks, gasping with cell phones out. The Rottweilers' jaws were slack, their tongues hanging out.

There was the car. It was flipped over, its front bumper crushed. Steam rose from the radiator, and it was leaking. The owner, stunned, stumbled out toward the sidewalk where bystanders caught him before he collapsed.

Blue barely had time to notice the fire before letting out a yelp and rushing to shield the puppies again.

BOOM! The small explosion engulfed her. She felt the heat surround her for a moment, and then it was over.

"That dog is mine," screamed a fat man in a stained T-shirt. He lunged toward her, trying to grab a clump of her fur as she nipped at him. Other people started rushing toward her, trying to pin her to the ground. She jumped out of the crowd and ran back to the pups, which were still trapped in the cage. This time when she grasped the cage's door, her teeth crushed the bars. Quickly grabbing the two small pups in her mouth, she sprinted down the alley at a speed so fast the sounds from that street were soon nothing but a dim whisper.

Once she got to her home, she gently dropped her new companions—two Labradors, one golden, one black.

CHAPTER 8

ROBO GROWLED IN FRUSTRATION. They had reached the bottom of the mountain, near the gas stations, barbecue huts, and flea markets of Jasper, Georgia. But when he tried to scale it with his robotic legs, he kept slipping on the wet granite. This was the fifth time he had failed to make the leap.

He howled with rage, and smacked his head into the rock in frustration. His pack looked at him, silent as mice, casting glances at each other.

They're scared. Even Savage is scared of me, Robo thought.

Robo felt another shudder of hatred and frustration, and he smashed his paw into the mountain's rock. The rock shattered into pieces, as if it had been glass. Robo felt a swell of his unnatural power. This time, he took a great leap—and made it over the ledge. He landed on his stomach—hard. He pulled himself up, and was able to easily scramble to the ridge.

He looked down on the pack, proud of himself and satisfied. The dogs looked terrified. Even Savage did, with his tail tucked between his legs. *They know what I can do with my power*, Robo thought, before scrambling to help them finish the climb.

"Don't just stand there! Let's keep moving!" Robo looked up, and saw the sun already halfway across the sky. They had stopped earlier to rest—the puppies were barely making it—and now they were late. He twitched his ear, signaling Savage to follow.

Finally, they came upon a plateau large enough to hold his

pack. Robo sniffed its boundaries. This would be a perfect place to set up camp at least for a night, if only the pack were not so easy to see, so exposed. Robo kept walking the edge though, looking for a trigger for old memories. Suddenly, he noticed a pile of rocks on the edge. *Strange.* Robo carefully sniffed around it—algae, Cheetos, and then…yes. The faint scent of humans from long ago. Quickly, he used his robotic legs to move the boulders. Savage and the rest of the dogs started to help.

He knew there was a passageway behind the rocks—a deep, dark tunnel. As the dogs peered in, there was no light except for the bright, red glow of Robo's mechanical eye.

As Robo walked deeper into the tunnel, he knew he had found the perfect home for his pack. *The humans will never, ever find us here. And if they do, it will turn out very badly for them.* He stopped in front of a massive steel door.

As the dogs huddled around him, Robo looked at the door, He wondered if there was a way to go around it. He then realized they didn't have to get around it. They could go through it.

The scientists had implanted a laser in his left shoulder, embedded in the metal plate. All he had to do was…

Turn. Laser. On.

As soon as he closed his eyes, he could hear the dogs gasp and scurry away from him. From his shoulder emerged an intense beam of red light that cut through the door.

Robo directed the light into a perfect circle. After a few minutes, he and Savage rammed the circle of metal with their paws until it fell inward into a room.

Sniffing the air, Robo crawled through first. As soon as he entered, he knew he had met his destiny.

With Savage by his side, Robo entered a massive auditorium. To the left and right of the floor were rivers of water; six cooling pipes feeding into these streams. There were three hallways that led to warehouses, secret rooms, offices, and laboratories filled with abandoned equipment, laptops, monitors, and cages.

Robo paused at the cage he realized had been his. He couldn't help shuddering.

"This is our new home," he said firmly, as Savage explored with him. "How fitting," he said with determination. "The humans will reap what they have sown."

When he returned to the auditorium, he found a hallway directly opposite the entrance.

Down the hall were three passageways, and as he and Savage explored, they found another set of steel doors. Behind those, Robo discovered the main control room, filled with monitors and wall-to-wall screens bolted directly into the granite bedrock of the mountain. In an adjoining room, catwalks were suspended over a pool of acid. Robo laughed bitterly, now understanding why it was there.

"The best way to get rid of evidence," he said bitterly to no one in particular.

Robo examined a series of large touchscreen monitors for clues. Within minutes, Robo had the security files with the compound's passwords and had turned on the fortress's massive power generator. With another swipe of his paw, he filled the room with light: the blue glow from the monitors.

As Robo surveyed the screens, one suddenly switched to a news report about a Husky—*that* Husky.

He and Savage watched her running to get the puppies.

They watched her get hit by a car, the car flipping over, gasoline leaking, and the small explosion.

Then, they watched her survive, running away from the scene, two puppies safely in her grip. As Savage murmured in amazement, Robo realized what this meant.

One of the scientists in Dexter's lab must have captured her—and then given the Husky powers as well.

To stop him. To end him.

And to think he had cared about her fate. That he had actually been worried that the humans had been unkind to her.

Robo's eye narrowed, and his lip curled. "CLAW!" he howled.

A huge gray and brown Mastiff lumbered up the stairs and to the control room to Robo, his tail down.

"Yep, boss?"

Robo lifted his paw to the video on the screen. "See that Husky?" he growled into Claw's ear. "I need you to go back to the city—and kill her."

CHAPTER 9

BLUE GENTLY SET THE PUPPIES DOWN.

"Thank you, thank you, thank you! " they yipped. "We love you, you're our friend." Eager to please, they licked her snout, their tiny tails wagging back and forth. One was a female, a black lab with a small patch of white on her ear. The other, a yellow male with oversized paws, seemed to glow with excitement.

Blue shifted her paws uncomfortably. She wasn't used to enthusiastic pups. For a moment she thought, *Maybe I can just leave them.* But she knew she couldn't just walk away.

She sighed. "Yeah, sure, whatever," she said, as she tried to get them out from under her legs, and herded them into the back of her den. Safe, the puppies fell asleep almost immediately.

In the morning, they woke her up by licking her nose and eyes.

"We're hungry, hungry, *hungry!*"

Blue rolled her eyes. But her own stomach was growling too, so she crawled out of the den to survey what might be available. The puppies wobbled after her.

Their first target: two boys eating burgers. Blue contemplated for a moment. "Maybe I should leave them with the boys. Boys like puppies, right?" She shook the idea out of her head as she watched the boys stabbing bugs with abandoned wire hangers.

Instead, Blue slowly stalked the boys, building up foam

around her mouth before she leaped out, looking fierce and terrifying, using "Rabies" again.

Surprised, they dropped their burgers and ran. Blue picked the burgers up, and dropped one in front of the puppies, who had been following behind her. The golden lab momentarily left it alone.

Spoiled brat. Blue started to growl. Both puppies only wanted to play, jumping and leaping on each other and Blue. In the midst of the play, one of them nipped her hard with sharp puppy teeth.

"Ow! You worthless ca-!" Blue cut herself off. Don't curse in front of the pups.

"Okay…both of you come here." The pups sat down, their floppy ears perked. "Let's get some things straight. Don't jump. Don't talk. Don't touch. Don't laugh. And don't bite."

The puppies cocked their heads, trying to pay attention. It didn't last long, and within seconds, one was biting the tail of the other, and they each started pushing around a tin can on the pavement. Blue let out another long sigh. "You know what? Never mind."

Later, herding them together, she tried a different tactic. "What are your names?"

"What's a name?" the golden one yipped.

Blue rolled her eyes again. *These pups are idiots.*

"Okay, you have a *name.* You have a *mother,"* she said in irritation. "You need to find her and annoy her instead." At her wit's end, she started pushing them down the alley with her snout. "Now go. I've given you food, get on home."

After nudging them to the sidewalk, she turned around to

catch a nap in her den.

The puppies trotted behind her. She glared at them. The golden puppy realized Blue wasn't playing.

"Please don't leave us right now," he whined. "We don't know where our mother is."

"Fine," Blue said. "Just don't annoy me."

Maybe their mother will come looking for them today. I'll stick it out with them just a few more hours.

Besides, as she watched them play with old potatoes and other trash from the alley, they were—well, cute. Okay, they were *really* cute.

As dusk approached, Blue realized that no one was coming for them. They, like her, were without a mom—alone. But she knew she was in no position to take care of two curious, careless babies in this world. Sadly, she knew reality would harden them soon.

However, watching them some more, her heart softened. She decided to take on this burden. But the moment they could care for themselves, they would have to go.

The three slept well that night, cuddled together, warm and happy.

The next morning, everyone was in a good mood. Blue maked sure the puppies understood their "territory," and went off to find food.

She came back, excited. Today, the coffee shop had dumped a bunch of gluten-free breakfast sandwiches in its dumpster. Apparently humans didn't love them as much as the shop owners thought they would.

As she turned the corner to the alley, she happily barked,

"Come here, fleabags! I've got food!"

She found them frozen in fear.

A mere foot away from them was a Mastiff on her turf. One she had never seen before.

He was missing an eye, with only a torn socket in its place, and had scars on his neck.

"Pups, run," snarled Blue.

The pups ran toward their den. Before Blue could give any more orders, the Mastiff charged her, slamming her to the pavement. She bit hard into the Mastiff's shoulder. She heard the puppies snarling and biting his legs with their sharp puppy teeth.

"Get off of me," the Mastiff howled before grabbing the black lab by the scruff and throwing her into the wall.

The puppy whimpered once, fell to the ground, and did not get up.

Something snapped in Blue. "Why, you CAT! I'll take out that other eye, you ONE-EYED CAT BRAIN!"

She felt a strange tingling in her muscles, as if every fiber of her being had suddenly come alive with power and strength.

Blue shoved him into the wall with an ease that startled her, slamming him with such force that the concrete began to crack.

Blue relaxed her grip, allowing the Mastiff to fall unconscious and limp to the ground.

She ran over to the pup still lying motionless on the ground. "Please don't die, don't die, don't die."

The pup turned her head toward Blue, and looked up at her, quiet and calm. She nuzzled Blue before sighing, and slowly closing her eyes.

Blue howled in rage. The golden lab, confused, tried to

comfort her. "She's just tired, and taking a nap," he said with big-eyed innocence.

"No, no, no! How can you be so stupid?" Blue snarled at him, before realizing he could not be expected to understand what had happened. She turned away briefly to regain her composure, and to try again. The male puppy now retreated in fear.

Blue softly called the puppy back. She and the puppy then found an abandoned coat near a dumpster, which she gently wrapped around the black puppy. Then she slid the wool coat into a brick alcove—hidden from the world, and safe from wind, rain, and the cold. It was peaceful and serene. It was the best she could do.

She called the golden lab over to her.

"I'm calling you Max," she said.

Looking down at the still body of his sister, tucked safely in the folds of wool, she said sadly, "And I'll call you Destiny."

PART 2

Red will rule the world,
And all with prints will suffer.

CHAPTER 10

ROBO STARED AT CLAW, shaking his head.

"Why are all of you so disappointing?" his voice boomed through the complex. Robo turned back toward the control room in disgust.

None of the dogs followed him. Instead they stood, shocked and hurt by his words.

He sat alone in the dimly lit room, frustrated and angry. He stared at the computer screens and a large, glowing globe showing a constant stream of satellite weather imaging and GPS data.

Calmer, Robo slipped into deep thought. He had to make these dogs stronger, smarter, and most importantly, give them a reason to fight the humans.

The dogs needed to return to their independent roots—to tap into the wolf in each of them, fiercely loyal to their own, deadly and cunning with their enemies.

But how?

He kicked the table in frustration, shaking the screens, and knocking a shredded can of chicken broth off the edge. Chicken broth was his favorite meal, a memory from his days with Becca. The can had been heated over the acid and, when it hit the floor, steam rose into the air.

His eyes brightened.

This was what he needed—something airborne that would

travel with the wind, custom-made just for dogs. Something to build his mighty army.

Robo finally had a plan.

For weeks, he isolated himself from his pack, which—despite its reservations about Robo's harsh words and odd behavior—liked its new home, with easy access to fresh water and food, and isolation from the world.

By this time, cold weather and ice had descended on the city. In the past, it had kept Robo's pack in a constant state of discomfort and illness, many dying from disease and starvation brought on by the hard conditions. But in the heart of the mountain, they were protected by the natural insulation of dirt and stone, and warmed by the activity, both electronic and animal. The pack was content, living off the stacks of food reserves the humans had left behind, sleeping in the cages, cozy now that Robo had stripped them of their locks. Savage, Robo's deputy, kept order and routine while Robo stayed deep in the shadows, staying up for days, planning and working. All the dogs were fed, but they also all had jobs to do; gathering food and water, cleaning the dens, watching the puppies. Most would go back to their dens feeling satisfied, secure, and useful.

Savage made sure Robo was also fed. He would assign the quietest of the dogs to slide cans of broth and meat quickly through the hole in the steel door of Robo's private quarters.

Savage still respected Robo—loved Robo—but late at night, as he curled up to sleep, Savage worried that something had changed in Robo, something that went beyond the additions of titanium and steel.

⅛

One day, Robo awoke and realized he needed a change of scenery. Majestically, he walked the halls, dogs scattering in his presence or staring in awe. His metallic paws clicked in rhythm on the floor. Briefly, he stopped to gently play with the new puppies, growling to their delight, and showing his shiny teeth, causing them to bound back and stand fiercely between their mothers' front legs.

His strength was back, his wounds healed. As he entered the massive auditorium, he could see his pack was working hard and thriving. He was pleased.

He climbed steel stairs to a platform where he could see all. With his massive paws hanging off the side of the platform, he lay down, tucking his head under his front leg. For the first time in months, Robo took a nap.

It was too short.

"Robo!"

Robo woke with a start, seeing dozens of dogs staring at him in fright.

"What do you want?" Robo growled, irritated again. He realized that the pack wasn't looking at him.

Robo whipped around and saw two men in white lab coats running up the stairs toward him. One, a young man, was armed with a syringe; the other, an old man with gray hair, had a strange monitor strapped to his arm.

Robo snarled and rushed toward one of the scientists.

His claws were outstretched, ready to slash and slay them, when he recognized the younger scientist. He had helped Dexter with Robo's genetic and robotic engineering.

Robo couldn't believe his luck. He knew what he needed to do.

His pack closed in on the humans, now huddled in the middle of the bridge hanging over acid. Savage walked up beside Robo, his teeth bared, ready to strike.

"I surrender, we surrender," the older man yelled. "Robo, we surrender."

Robo shook his head; it had been a while since he had heard human words, as "Homosapien's language: English" clicked across the bottom of his robotic eye's grid.

The man turned around, raising his hands in the air as more dogs crowded the entrance, growling and snarling. He turned back to Robo and took a deep breath.

"Robo, you need to come back with us," the older man said, his voice shaking. "We need to make adjustments in your programs."

Robo raised his eyebrow; a metallic grin crept across his face. He burst into laughter—a deep, bitter laugh, raspy and loud.

"You really think you can convince me to come with you?" Robo laughed again, speaking precise English to the men, which caused them both to gasp in surprise.

Then, he rose to his full height, giving them a dead, cold stare.

"Oh no, no, no. You're staying with *me*," Robo said, signaling to Savage to make sure a tight ring of dogs now surrounded the two scientists. The older scientist, overwhelmed with his fear of Robo and his pack, sank to his knees. Robo's eye scanned the man's vital signs, flashing "heart rate: dangerous," before the man fell against the railing of the bridge.

Robo's eye registered no heartbeat. The man did not move.

The younger man, also terrified, tried to scramble away from the still body of his colleague. But he was met with the growling, snarling teeth of the dogs.

Robo stepped forward through the pack, and spoke to the man.

"Only one left," he said. "You're the one I wanted anyway. Remember me? Remember what you did? Well, now, you are going to help me," he hissed as the man tried to crawl away from him, avoiding the red glow of Robo's eye. "You are going to give my dogs some of the same powers you have given me."

Leaning close to the man, his nostrils flaring, Robo whispered, "And if you don't, you will be thrown to the…wolves," with a deep laugh.

"Take him to a cage," he turned and barked to Savage.

The dogs immediately started dragging the scientist toward the cages, while he screamed, "Don't kill me! Don't kill me. Please don't kill me."

A Doberman from the pack stepped toward Robo.

"Yes?" Robo asked sternly.

"What should we do with the body?" asked the Doberman.

"What is your name?"

"Sabu. Here to serve," the young Doberman said proudly.

"Good," said Robo. "Push it into the river, and let it float back to the city as a warning."

"A warning for whom?" Sabu asked.

"For humans," Robo sneered. "Not that they'll notice."

Sabu and a few others grabbed the body and dragged it out of the compound. The other scientist watched in horror from his own cage.

When Sabu returned, he approached Robo again.

Robo was getting tired of this young upstart.

"What now?"

"In three months, I'm supposed to check in with a traveler named Buddy."

Robo rolled his eyes. "Why are you wasting my time, soldier?"

"Well, it appears Buddy is the old friend of a certain dog... A certain Husky," Sabu said, backing up slightly. "A Husky I believe you're interested in, from what Savage says. I could make sure he brings her along," Sabu lowered his voice.

Robo smiled.

"Sounds like a plan," he said. "Good job...lieutenant."

Sabu bowed to Robo, and went to make preparations for his trip.

Robo returned to the bridge.

"Splat! Unknown!" he bellowed.

The two dogs jumped into the auditorium, and sprinted through the steel doors to the control room.

Facing Robo, they cocked their ears for instruction. Robo quickly outlined Sabu's connections, and why they were needed. "We can accomplish two things with one trip: Find the orb and get that Husky."

CHAPTER 11

BLUE HATED WINTER IN THE CITY. Curled next to Max to keep him warm, Blue spent most of her time in their makeshift den. She left only to eat and drink. Gray bleakness filled most of the days until a rare ice storm, followed by snow, caused everything in Georgia to come to a grinding stop.

The air was silent and crisp. She caught a familiar scent, followed by a familiar bark.

"Hello?" a voice howled in the frozen wind. Blue raised her head and perked her ears.

A German Shepherd was staring at her, with a big toothy grin.

"Buddy!" Blue said joyously. She crawled out. Max followed.

"Who is it?" Max asked, sleepily, staring at the dog breathing clouds of steam in the fresh snow.

Blue looked at her long-time friend with fondness. Over the years, Buddy had visited her and Diamond each winter, coming back from all points of the world. He came from a long line of traveling dogs, packs that would forage from city to city. These bands of dogs learned about different cultures, and often picked up tricks and survival techniques with every new pack they met. Of course, sometimes the packs would find things missing days or weeks after the traveling band left—but it was *almost* okay because of the glitter and mystery the new dogs brought.

To Blue, Buddy always made the world brighter, especially when her small life in the alley was gray and cold.

Piercings were in his ears. In addition, she noticed tattoos on his stomach where the hair was less dense. Strange symbols she didn't recognize.

"New markings?" she asked, one eye raised.

"Yeah," Buddy said, "I found a whole new clan of dogs hidden among the Pyramids."

Max peeked out between Blue's two front legs.

"Soooo. You've had a pup?" Buddy lowered his big head to Max.

"Oh, no, no. Nothing like that," Blue said. "I saved him from being hit by a car."

Buddy nodded. He looked around her den, sniffing. Not much there.

Blue smiled. "Please," she said, waving her paw in a grand jesture, "join me for some rat."

Buddy laughed. "Ah, yes, you're just the most elegant of dogs."

They talked and laughed for hours.

As it got darker, Buddy changed the conversation. "Blue," he said. "I almost completely forgot. There is going to be an even bigger snowstorm than this." He disdainfully pressed into the snow where it only came up to his knee.

"You need to come with me to safety, especially now that you have this pup."

Annoyed, Blue said, "Well, thanks for telling me." She started to look worried. Their home was not faring well in the cold, with the snow slowly banking around it.

Buddy shrugged. "Sorry, I was distracted by your lovely rat dinner. Chin up; we've still got time. But we have to get a move on."

"I can bring Max too, right?" she asked.

"Of course!" he said. "Let's get out of here. I've already got a truck in mind."

᭟

The truck was perfect. It was filled with snow-covered firewood, the perfect camouflage for him and Blue. A tarp covered everything. With a quick yip, Buddy, Max, and Blue climbed under a big tarp beside a small stack of wood, warm and safe.

"I don't really feel like making a run for any more wood today," a bearded red-haired man said to another, shorter version. "It's bound to get worse out there, and you know, Atlanta don't know nothing about snow," he said with a laugh. "I just want to get back home, with a quilt, a beer, and a video game controller."

He paused. "Oh, and my family—always forget that." Both men chuckled.

"You're funny, but we need at least two more cords of wood. It's time to make the money," the short man said. "So it's time to get hauling."

He blew the steam off his warm cup of coffee. "Get back into those mountains, pick up that firewood, and then get the heck home. We just gotta get the job done as quick as possible."

The red-haired man grumbled, put on an orange sock hat, and cranked up the truck. "Too dang old for this."

The truck headed off with the dogs on board, rumbling and crunching through the thin layer of snow and ice.

Blue hoped things would be better where they were going, especially for Max. She snuggled in with the other two for the long ride ahead.

❧

Blue hadn't realized she had fallen asleep, until Buddy nudged her awake the next morning.

"This is it," he said in short barks. "We need to get out here."

Once Buddy saw the red-haired man walk away, the three leaped from the truck. Landing silently in the deep, soft snow, they ran toward a grove of trees.

Blue stood for a moment, taking in the vista of mountains before her. They were round, gentle slopes of land, covered in trees and snow—silent. Coming from the city, this quiet was almost unnerving.

She realized she could smell dogs—many of them. Yet, she didn't see any. Only a rolling field with...

"Snow dens," Buddy said with joy. "*Most* Huskies know how to build snow dens as insulation from the cold." Blue knew he was gently mocking her. "It will keep you and Max safe through the storm."

Suddenly, dogs burst out of the snow, yipping, barking, and bounding toward them.

Buddy walked up to the pack's leader, Balta, a white Husky and clearly the Alpha of the snow pack. Buddy bowed to her. "I have brought Blue as we discussed, but will you also offer protection to this pup, Max?"

"Anything for you, Buddy, but they will have to prepare with the rest of us. The storm is set to get much worse. All of you will probably have to stay here at least one night."

Balta barked to her captains to show Blue and Max how to form their own snow den. After Max wore himself out leaping in the snow and eating a full meal of deer meat, Blue and Max snuggled together again for another restful night.

The next day, a blizzard hit the mountains, howling through the forest. Even inside Blue's den, wind pushed against her newly formed walls, making her shiver. Max was sneezing, and Blue worried that his nose was dry. She feared she hadn't made a very good snow den. After all, even Buddy had declined to share it with her. Instead, he'd made his own den elsewhere.

The entire day had been cold. The fact that it would've been worse in Atlanta kept her going—no help, no shelter, no knowledge to protect against this onslaught of ice. It felt like a thousand hours had passed since she had woken up this morning. Exhaustion got the best of her, and she settled Max down. He fell asleep quickly, and she curled around him and slowly nodded off.

Late that night, Blue awoke to murmuring sounds far away. Her ears pricked as she tried to detect the voices. She whispered to Max, "Stay here," before slowly crawling out of her now cozy and warm snow den, carefully keeping it intact for the puppy.

On the ground with her eyes barely peeking above the snow, her white fur was a perfect cover. Two dogs were whispering to each other.

"I have brought the Husky as promised," Buddy quietly told a Doberman Blue did not recognize.

"Good," the Doberman replied.

"I expect my reward soon," Buddy said, starting to circle back to his den. "Remember—don't hurt her or the pup. I like them both."

"Yeah, there's been a change in plans about that," the Doberman said, with a sudden snarl. Buddy turned toward him and swerved his head, but the Doberman sprang forward, ripping a deep wound into his throat, splattering blood onto the white snow.

Blue couldn't comprehend what she had just seen. It happened so fast, like a knife cutting her own heart. Her eyes started to burn hot with tears, but instead of howling in grief, she stayed still—her survival instincts taking over.

The Doberman sniffed the air, and said to himself, "Where's that Husky?" His eyes suddenly brightened, and with one leap, he plowed through her den and stepped back out with Max in his jaws.

Blue couldn't bear it any more.

"Hey, JERK!" she barked.

The Doberman squinted trying to see the white and black dog against the white snow and black night. He dropped Max in the snow and laughed. "Blue. That is your name, right? I'm going to need you to come with me. Otherwise, well…things are going to get much worse." He leaned close to the terrified pup, the blood of Buddy still on his fur.

Blue felt her fur rising and ears move backwards. "You pick on puppies? What a coward. What scum."

Sabu rolled his eyes. *Why does every job have to become so difficult.*

Pushing Max to side, he lunged at Blue, knocking her down. She hit her head on a rock buried beneath the snow. Blue scrambled to her feet, ears ringing from the rock.

"Is that all you've got?" she yelled.

Sabu narrowed his eyes. Blue sprang at him, but he was quicker and dodged her. She wasn't used to this snow, despite being a Husky. She regrouped, shaking off the snow trapped in her coat. Snarling again, Blue tried to catch him, but once again missed. This time he pushed her to the ground and pinned her there. Blue struggled under him, snapping at his paws.

"Let me go, you fool!"

Sabu laughed, "Fool? Take a look at a mirror once in a while!"

For a split second, the Doberman seemed distracted.

"What's that?" Sabu asked. "Oh, sorry. Okay, I got it."

Blue realized that, while he was momentarily distracted by what seemed to be imaginary voices, he had shifted his weight on her. She quickly slid out from under him, and kicked him hard in the jaw with her back legs. He fell back, something flying from his ear.

Blue got to her feet. He was lying still on the cold ground, breathing slowly. Her kick had injured his nose and mouth; blood stained the snow. Blue walked over to the black device that had been clipped to his pointed ear. She sniffed it, and very faintly, she heard a voice coming from it.

WHAM!

Blue fell forward from the impact, her vision blurred. The Doberman stood over her, breathing heavily. She tried to get up, but the earth began spinning.

She snarled at him: "Take one more step, and you're dead, cat breath."

The Doberman watched her try to burrow deeper into the snow for protection. "Get on your feet and show me what you've got," he sneered.

Blue was defeated. She knew it. She couldn't even raise her head.

Sabu slipped the earphone back on. "Yeah, she's still alive. I'm sure she's fine. She's got a thick skull."

Blue muttered at him as she faded out: "Shut...up...cat breath."

The Doberman smacked Blue with his huge paw.

A dog was coming closer to her. A German Shepherd, with thick brown and black fur. Blue moaned in pain. Buddy, is that you? The German Shepherd stood there for a second in silence, staring at her. Slowly, he shook his head. "No. Dig deeper," he whispered to her. Then, he slowly turned and walked away, disappearing into the snowstorm. She looked up one more time, and he became a ghost against the gray horizon.

Blue blacked out. As her head dropped into the blood-stained snow a final time, one small pierced hoop caught in her paw.

CHAPTER 12

BLUE WOKE UP, STARTLED. She was back in her old den, slightly damp from melted snow. Everything ached. She immediately looked around for Max, but only found a tablet tucked in with her. She instantly knew what it was—she had watched humans for years, playing with them and swiping at them. Humans loved these things.

So when she saw the sign of a gear with a dog in it, she swiped at it. A video began to play. The first thing that flashed on the screen—that she found she could *read*—was RAD: Robotic Association of Dogs.

She heard his voice. "Hello, Blue."

The screen was black except for one bright, red sphere in the middle of the screen. She shivered.

"Blue, I'm your new best friend."

She rolled her eyes.

"I'm Robo, leader of RAD. Before I get to the point, I simply must apologize for the way my lieutenant, Sabu, treated you. It was planned to be a much less...traumatic affair. You did put on quite the fight, though, against a Doberman. I'm slightly impressed. So, no hard feelings, okay?"

Robo's deep voice continued. "You might have noticed by now that you've been given a very special...gift. I'm sure you have noticed that you're smarter, stronger, and faster. That's good news for both of us."

Robo paused, the eye's clicking pupil focusing and refocusing.

"I have a proposition for you. You can help me get something I want, and I'll return something you want. First, what I want."

The screen lit up with a video of a scientist holding up a strange, glowing blue orb. Blue watched him use the orb in a series of tests of greater and greater destructive power.

This orb was like nothing she had ever seen.

"And now, something you want."

Another video flashed on the screen—tiny Max whimpering in a cage. "Blue, BLUE! HELP ME!" he howled.

Robo's voice was now menacing. "Choose carefully." He cleared his throat. "I'll be sending two...um...*escorts* to pick you up soon. Don't waste this opportunity. You won't get another one."

The message ended.

Blue sat there frozen, overwhelmed, and confused.

She paced the alley. How did she get back home? Most importantly, why should she go with these dogs?

She almost chose not to. Nothing good had happened since she'd taken in those puppies: nothing but struggle and death. They had made her an easy target. They had made her vulnerable.

She crossed her paws in front of her, and noticed the hoop caught on her claw.

Did Buddy betray her? She had to know. Surely he wouldn't do that to her, do that to Max. Poor Max. He'd already lost his mother and his sister. She remembered how he had whined at night from his terrible memories, and she had placed her paw over him to comfort him. She remembered how the only true happiness she had had in recent weeks was playing with that silly puppy. He had been overjoyed in the alley with tin cans and old hot dogs. Overjoyed in the snow, even as it made him shiver and shake. Overjoyed everywhere, just as long as he was with her.

Blue hung her head. She *hated* feeling this way—*hated* having someone rely on her. She would rather not trust anyone, and have no one trust her. It was easier. Right now, Blue just wanted to leave; leave the alley and all the bad memories behind.

But again, she decided not to do what she wanted to do. She would meet this Robo, and rescue Max.

※

As the sun rose high in the sky, two dogs showed up in Blue's alley.

"My name is Splat," said the Australian Shepherd. "You know why we're here."

The other dog was a skinny, gray dog with short, floppy ears and a crooked snout. She seemed to be a mixed breed of many bloodlines, but mostly Greyhound. Blue didn't trust either of them; it was instinct.

The skinny dog noticed Blue staring.

"My name is Unknown," she said quickly. "Take this bag; we've got work to do."

Feeling hopeless, Blue padded after them. As they twisted and turned through the streets, the city became shabbier and more dangerous.

"So, who's this Robo?" Blue asked to Unknown's visible irritation. The Grayhound only responded: "He's a great leader."

Finally, they stopped in front of a rusted metal door.

"We're here," said Splat.

He reared up on his back legs and easily pushed the door inward. Inside, they were in a lab similar to the one where Blue had been collared. The three also spotted a worker in a white lab coat, his back to them. Splat lunged at the man and knocked him unconscious.

"Get a move on," Unknown said, as she jabbed Blue. Blue snarled at her.

The three finally stopped in front of a large vault door unlike anything Blue had seen. Unknown sighed, annoyed. "I'll be right back," she said, and limped down the hall. She returned with a keycard that had been on the worker.

"Robo said you'd know what to do." Splat pushed the keycard to Blue. To her surprise, Blue realized she did. She had seen the scientists use this before. Slowly, she swiped it through the scanner with her mouth. Nothing. She leaned forward to see what was wrong, and realized the security camera was scanning her eye. A "retinal scan"—as precise and unique as a human's fingerprint. She must have been scanned and registered while captured—just like the scientists who worked there.

The three jumped back as they heard locks and bolts pull back as the vault opened. Splat, Unknown, and Blue stepped into the massive steel room, completely empty except for one clear case with a strange, blue, glowing orb inside.

It almost looks like blue fire, Blue thought, *the same color as my eyes.* Unknown pushed her toward the case.

"Open the bag, cat," Unknown muttered to Blue.

Unknown then shoved the case and the orb into the bag and put the bag over her shoulder.

"Let's go," she growled, breaking into a run.

Hearing the pounding of humans' feet toward the vault, the three ran out, dodging examining tables and equipment. They finally climbed out some low, broken windows that disguised the building to look like just one more abandoned building. Once near the street, Splat and Unknown moved unseen into the bushes. Blue, not knowing a better option, began to do the same, until she noticed they were approaching a main road out of the city.

Her head suddenly started pounding. Blue's eyes rolled back, and she started to seize.

There was only the glow of one huge monitor that filled a wall. A grotesque Great Dane with metal body parts was in the center of the room, placing a flaming orb into its titanium case. "They will pay for what they did to me. What they have done to us. They will all DIE." He shut the case, walked over to a holographic display, and slowly typed a long code with his paw. Suddenly, dozens of monitors came to life with live feeds from all over the world showing explosions, buildings, trees, and people burned to ash. Blue watched it all in terror, her heart pounding.

Blue opened her eyes. She was still on the street. The other two dogs were calling her to hurry, to get into the bushes. In the street, Blue saw cars screeching to a halt, heard sirens, and smelled burned rubber—an accident right in the main intersection. She didn't want to hide in bushes; there were much better options.

Glancing around, she saw a high dumpster—perfect! She positioned herself and waited.

Within seconds, a dozen police cars had arrived. Panicked

by the sudden influx of humans near the bushes, Unknown and Splat tried to bury the orb and run—with a plan to circle back around. But Blue watched their every move. Just as she had experienced in the past, Unknown and Splat were quickly collared by two police officers, so the others could concentrate on the wreck without stray dogs in the way.

Blue saw her chance to retrieve the bag. Quickly, she jumped down, dug it out and slung it over her shoulder. Then, running along the sidewalks, and then later, the grass and gravel lane along the highway—she headed out of Atlanta, determined to find where Max might have been taken. Eventually, she was far from the city and into the heart of the rural South.

There was suddenly no humans or dogs in sight—and no scent. She was lost.

After hours on the road, she retreated into some piles of pine straw, dug a bed, and lay down in a tight circle. Sleep did not come easily.

CHAPTER 13

"THE MISSION *FAILED*?" Robo swung his large head towards Splat. "I'm sorry," he said very slowly and with sarcasm. "What *exactly* does that mean?"

Splat looked down at his paws, scared. "The Husky—Blue. She has the orb."

Robo's eye widened with rage. He raised his robotic paw and slashed the claws across Splat's cheek. Robo gritted his teeth, breathing hard. His head and ears were down, and his shoulders hunched.

Splat quickly rolled to expose his stomach in submission, praying that Robo would not kill him. After all, he had gotten them both out of the pound—two more dogs who escaped Harold's grasp.

Instead, Robo turned his head to Unknown in anger, who tried to take a step back, her torn ears down, and her short tail under her legs. Robo felt his muscles tighten.

"I GIVE YOU A HOME, AND THIS IS WHAT I GET IN RETURN?" Robo howled in frustration, his natural eye crazed and his robotic eye flickering. Splat slowly crawled away from him, shaking.

"Get out…" Robo snarled. "GET OUT!"

Unknown and Splat fled the control room, brushing past Sabu, who was walking in.

"Sir!" Sabu said crisply.

"What?" Robo spat, his back facing the young Doberman.

"I didn't want to interrupt your…meeting," Sabu said carefully. "But the scientist has finally created—" he lowered his voice, "what you need."

Robo turned around, ears pricked up.

Sabu proudly led Robo through the steel doors of a large laboratory. The scientist was startled, and instinctively backed against the wall as Robo walked into the room.

It had taken months for Robo to win over scientist Dr. John Fox, one of the three from Dr. Rune's laboratory. Convincing him to continue his work took a combination of long conversations and large amounts of money. The money had been stolen from criminals' bank accounts around the world, which Robo had hacked. Stealing from thieves, liars, and drug dealers actually brought Robo great joy. It was definitely worth it.

Over broth and green tea—John's favorite—the scientist started to open up to Robo about how he had been recruited by Dexter. Robo learned about the scientists' work before his fiery escape from Dr. Rune's lab. John told Robo that it hadn't seemed to be a bad endeavor—a way for him to work with extraordinary dogs who would be the new weapon of the 21st century: nimble, smart, and, yes, sometimes expendable.

It was also a way for him to make a comfortable living.

The chats, of course, were for John more than Robo. Robo only loved John for one reason: he was brilliant, which Robo could use.

Just as importantly, John believed in Robo's plan for how the future should go; though, he had no idea how far Robo intended to take it.

"Robo!" John said, cheerfully. Robo was always slightly irritated with how little respect humans showed other species, even if they liked them.

"John," Robo said sternly. "I hear you have something to show me."

"Yes, I do," John said proudly. "It's ready. Come look."

Unknown and Splat entered the room, Sabu behind them. Robo's eye twitched as he tried to control his anger.

"Are you ready?" John asked, as he rubbed the two dogs behind the ears. "Unknown and Splat, why don't you hop in there," he said in a too-cheery voice, pointing to a glass holding-pen.

They looked at him suspiciously, ears cocked, but too afraid of Sabu and Robo to argue.

John checked his new monitor, strapped to his wrist. Slowly, he poured a mustard-yellow serum into a glass tube, which ran into a closed, stainless steel bowl. Underneath the bowl, there was a heat ring that caused the serum to boil, and a mist slowly rose, carried by an air stream into the glass pen.

Unknown and Splat initially looked alarmed, but when they found they could still breathe, they lay down and relaxed.

John checked his monitor, and turned everything off.

"Come on out, Unknown and Splat," he called, as he unlocked the glass tank.

They stared at him in shock. They somehow felt stronger and smarter.

"What has happened to us?" Unknown asked, shivering in awareness.

"You have become part of the new ruling class," Robo said

with a smile. "Well done, John Fox. You get to live another day."

John laughed, and then hesitated when Robo failed to join him.

"So, are we ready?" Robo asked.

John nodded his head. "I think so."

"Then start it. Start it now."

A week later, the two—one smart human and and one genius Great Dane—walked into the control room together. They lowered a vat of the yellow serum over the hot acid pit. Like the heat ring, the acid slowly brought the serum to a boil, and a mist filled the room.

Robo threw open the steel door of the control room. Huge fans pushed the smoke into the open auditorium. He howled for Savage and Sabu to gather the dogs in the auditorium, which was now filled with the strange mustard-yellow mist.

Within an hour, the mountain compound was filled with a new kind of dog. Strong, fast, and powerful. And, most importantly to Robo, oh-so-smart.

***

A month later, Robo was ready to unveil his plan.

Slowly, he climbed up to his platform, his metal feet clanking on the steel stairs. Staring down, he addressed his pack.

"It is time to take back what is rightfully ours, " he said, his red eye glowing. "Our dignity.

"Humans have done horrible things to us. They have killed tens of thousands of our babies—litters tossed away or killed in shelters. They have tortured and killed our strong brothers in fight clubs. They have run our beautiful sisters to death on racetracks. They eat us like cattle in China, Korea, and Vietnam. They breed our mothers to death." He paused momentarily, the memory of his own mother breaking his concentration.

Robo regained his composure: "And now they are using us in their terrible, terrible experiments for war."

He leaned forward, making eye contact with the dogs in the front row.

"Look at me. *Look at me*," he said. "Look what they have done. This must stop. They must be stopped."

The dogs howled in unison, snarling and growling as they remembered the cruelty each had endured from humans. "Stop them," they howled. "Stop them now. Stop them NOW. Stop them NOW," they chanted.

Even Robo was surprised by the enthusiasm and intensity of his pack. He had almost forgotten how many dogs had suffered. One of his former friends, Raven, had come running to him for help after had seen his mother beaten to death by a gang of humans. Robo never forgot how desperate and sad Raven was.

"John Fox," Robo commanded. "Begin."

John had been leaning against the wall, trying not to be noticed. But now, he carefully stepped forward and began pouring the serum into the vats throughout the complex. With the help of Robo's officers, he turned on a powerful ventilation system that started pushing billions of particles into the mountain air.

The dogs barked in triumph as they watched the mist drift through the air.

Happy and tired, Robo sent the pack back to their dens. He went back to his glowing globe, touching it and watching the weather patterns around the world.

"The winds of fate," he said under his breath.

Exhausted, he retired to his own den. He first took a detour to visit a golden Lab puppy caged in an isolated room. The puppy's fur was tangled, and his eyes were wet from tears. It reminded him of Savage when he was a pup. This Lab has much potential.

The puppy growled as the Robo sat next to the cage.

"Where is Blue?" the puppy asked with as much bravado as he could muster.

"Oh, sweet boy," Robo said smoothly. "She's on her way. I have no doubt she'll come for you."

The puppy snarled, "You're not going to win, you meanie."

Robo laughed. With one last stare into the cage, he double-checked the lock and walked toward his den.

CHAPTER 14

BLUE'S STOMACH RUMBLED, and she stared down at it, annoyed. *Why do you always complain?*

She had been walking for days in terrain she didn't recognize without any sign of Splat, Unknown, or Max.

Now in a large meadow, Blue's head barely peered over the tall grass. "I guess I need to hunt or something," she muttered to herself. She thought about the hunting shows she had seen through store windows—there were lots of gun shops in her part of town. Men in furry hats were always sprinting through fields with their dogs barking, causing ducks to fly out of the grass or off the lake. The dogs on those shows, usually labs like Max, were always walking around with dead ducks in their mouth.

Yum. Duck.

Blue started jumping around the meadow, breaking sticks, stirring leaves, and splashing in a nearby creek. *This will definitely help me find ducks, which will then fly into my mouth, like salmon to bears*, she thought. Hours later, she began to realize that this technique was not working. She sat down, hot, tired, and, of course, still hungry.

I don't get it, what am I doing wrong?

After a full day without eating, instinct finally took over. She stayed low to ground, her tail flat, her padded feet helping her move silently through the brush. She narrowed her eyes, finally spotting a large raccoon. It twitched its head at Blue, and she felt anger crawl up her spine. The raccoon almost seemed like it was taunting her. *Keep your head low, don't be intimated,* she thought. Slowly Blue sunk into the tall grass, and slunk past a rotting tree. The raccoon still sat there, ruffling its fur with its tiny hands, and glaring at her. Blue prepared to pounce, when a growl echoed through the field, and a flash of gray flew past her. Something had tackled the raccoon.

Blue took a step back into the tall grass in surprise.

"You stupid spy!" the coyote snarled at the raccoon, tearing it apart and flinging clumps of fur into the air. When Blue looked closer, the racoon didn't appear to be an animal at all, but a machine. Sparks flew around it as the coyote ripped off its paws, and bolts fell to to the ground.

Blue slowly started to back away, snapping a large stick in the process. The coyote lifted his head, staring in her direction. *Oh, come on,* Blue thought, frustrated. She turned and starting running full speed.

The coyote chased after her, but Blue had distance on her side. She ran blindly with her head down until she noticed too late that she was going to run straight into a tree. Blue tried to stop, but instead, she slid in muck around the tree. She hit it straight on with such force, a dangling, large branch fell on her, trapping her in the water and mud.

Blue, in pain, tried to keep quiet as she heard the coyote moving toward her. Finally, the coyote spoke from somewhere closeby, "Sure, I can spot the raccoon that's a camera, but not a dog. Gotta work on that."

Right then, he noticed the broken branch with Blue sinking beneath it.

"Wow, I almost thought you got away," he said in an almost friendly tone—until he saw her bag. Suddenly, he turned around and walked back into the tall grass.

"You're not going to leave me here, are you? Are you such a coward that you won't fight me like a real coyote?" Blue howled after him, hoping to lure him back to get the branch off of her.

The coyote chuckled softly. "I'll be back, Fuzzy Wuzzy."

Blue strained her ears. He was still talking.

"Yes, we have a Code Six here. She appears to be a straggler," the coyote said. "Yes. It's serious. Could you please stop singing? You're out of tune anyway." He paused. "Yes, well, she has the mark and was close to one of the cameras. No. No, I'm not. I'm not touching her. She might activate some laser or something—who knows?"

Blue narrowed her eyes. Apparently she had found an insane coyote who was hearing voices, and was certainly not going to help her with the branch.

"Fine, fine, I'll keep her here. Just get here quick."

The coyote walked back toward Blue. She stopped trying to lift the branch, and decided to try to charm him.

"Hey, there," she awkwardly tried to smile.

The coyote looked perplexed. She looked weird.

"We got off on the wrong paw," Blue said, giving up on the whole charm thing. "I'm a scout for my pack, and they're on their way. That's, um…" she didn't know what the normal number for a pack was, "like twenty-five dogs who are going to come rescue me."

The coyote took a step back.

"So you better help me get this branch off before that

happens, so I can put in a good word for you," she said.

"Nope."

"What?"

"Nope. You're staying put, Fuzzy Wuzzy. I've got a Code Six on you."

Blue rolled her eyes.

The coyote sat down, staring at Blue. She felt uncomfortable in the silence, and tried to start a conversation. "So, what's your story?"

The coyote turned his head. "I'm not talking to you, Fuzzy Wuzzy. RAD members will exploit any kind of weakness."

Blue looked to the ground. Where did she hear RAD before?

"Come on. It seems, being in the position I'm in, it really won't matter."

The coyote sighed. He was bored. It was hot. The only sound in the meadow was the buzz of cicadas.

"Okay. My name is Rex and I w—"

Suddenly, a huge flash of brown fur leaped in front of Rex.

"Naaaaw!" the brown dog howled, whacking Rex with a long brown paw. "You hush right now. You flat out talk too much. I'm fixin' to just wrap that mouth with duct tape."

The newcomer was a massive Bloodhound with long ears, a long snout, and a strong southern accent. He sat down in front of her, next to Rex. Both of them watched her struggle under the branch.

"On the other hand, she must not be too smart, huh?" the Bloodhound said to Rex.

Rex replied, "Yep, any dog so dumb to run smack into a tree—well, the porch light's on, but nobody's home."

"She's so dumb, that if she threw herself on the ground, she'd miss," the Bloodhound cracked.

They both broke into loud laughter. Blue was furious.

The Bloodhound became serious, and stepped closer to Blue.

"So, what do we really have here," he sniffed at her and the bag.

Blue snarled, "Get this branch off of me!"

The Bloodhound turned to Rex. "I do believe she's throwing a hissy fit."

Rex was preoccupied, talking again to himself. "I told you this is a Code Six—we have a straggler. She might have something to do with these dang animal cams. She was right next to one."

The Bloodhound turned back to Blue.

"Okay, let's get down to business. Tell us about these animal cams. And tell us more about you, Fuzzy Wuzzy."

She lost her temper. "My name is BLUE, you CAT!"

"She is madder than a wet hen," the Bloodhound said, amused. "She sure ain't no robot. In fact, she's kind of cute when she's mad." He went over to her, and licked her nose. "You so cute, Fuzzy Wuzzy."

Blue kept straining against the branch. *Where are my powers?* she thought in frustration.

"So what's the deal with the animal cams, city girl?" the Bloodhound asked.

Blue looked at him.

"You are so barking up the wrong tree," she snarled. "I have no idea what you're talking about. I'm just a lost dog who's looking for a puppy."

"You lie like a rug," the Bloodhound said, his good nature disappearing. "Do you think we didn't notice your bag marked with RAD?"

RAD. Uh-oh. Blue had completely forgotten that the bag holding the orb had the initials on it, along with the stamp of a gear and a dog. This could be bad.

"I was forced to steal this," she said, earnestly. "By a strange dog—Robotic, Robot, Robo—it was Robo!"

Rex snickered. "The mighty Robo. I prefer to call him Lego—all those different parts."

The Bloodhound silenced him. He then walked back to Blue, sniffing at the bag.

"Let's start over. My name is Copper, and I'm going to take a leap of faith with you and tell you the truth. I'm a general in the Secret Association of Dogs, or SAD."

Blue looked at him.

"You're kidding, right?" she asked. "SAD? That's like the worst name ever."

Copper laughed deeply. "Yep, missy, it really is. It doesn't make for a great dog tag either." His voice wandered. "But if you have the orb, things could be a lot different for SAD."

Blue pulled the bag closer. "No way. Why would I give it to you?"

"Well, you're probably still hankering to get free to start. But, I'm sure a smart girl like you has got this all figured out. You know, with your twenty-five-dog pack and all." Copper turned away. "C'mon Rex, we'll just wait for her to die and then we'll get the bag."

Rex looked at her one last time. "There's a tree stump in

Louisiana with a higher IQ."

Copper started talking to himself now. "Message AlphaGem, we have located the orb. Repeat. We have located the orb."

They walked into the high grass and lay down for an afternoon nap.

Blue knew this was her only chance. Her back legs were bruised, and she was sore from the branch, but she had to get it off of her and get free.

All I have to do is tap into that strength, she thought. *I stopped a car, for Dog's sake. Surely I can lift a branch.*

She closed her eyes and focused on the branch. "Power up!" she yelled.

Nothing happened. She could hear laughing in the meadow.

Angry, she did it again. "Power UP!"

Nothing. She could barely breathe now with the full weight of the branch on her chest.

"Are you done, Fuzzy Wuzzy?" Copper asked, re-emerging from the grass. "It's pretty clear you're not a robot, so I don't know why you think you've got some 'on' switch, like that no-good raccoon."

Blue stayed silent.

"So lemme get this straight. You say you're looking for a puppy. You say that Robo forced you to steal the orb. You say you're one of the good guys," he said. "Yet, you're so nasty you could make a preacher cuss. And even though you're going to die under that branch within a few days, you're clinging on to that bag and that orb you don't even really care about. Tell me, Blue, what's your story?"

Blue panted in the noonday sun. She *was* lost. She had an

orb that everyone wanted, but she didn't even know what it did. Copper certainly didn't seem as bad as Robo, and Rex—well, Rex was just annoying. However, they clearly either knew where Robo was, or at least how to track him down, which means she might be able to find Max again.

She too was going to have to take a leap of faith and trust Copper.

Squinting her eyes, she finally looked Copper in the eye.

"Okay, Floppy Bunny, you win," she said. "Help get this branch off of me, and help me find my puppy, and we'll talk about this orb. Deal?"

He laughed. "Floppy Bunny? That's *my* new nickname? Sure, Blue, we got a deal."

Copper and Rex lifted the branch and dragged her out of the muck. Blue thought she might make a break for it, but her legs immediately collapsed under her, and she found she could only limp slowly.

"Floppy Bunny," Rex snorted at Copper. "I think she's got you pinned."

"You hush, Rex," Copper said with a chuckle, and he began to sing a country song under his breath.

CHAPTER 15

CLOVER SAT DOWN, looking at his empty water dish. A Saint Bernard, Clover was a brown and white dog with green eyes. Huge, but harmless, his tongue lolled from his mouth as he saw his youngling walking toward him, holding a tin bucket of water.

Clover jumped up on him with just enough force to convey how absolutely excited he was to see him, but not hard enough to push him over. This was his boy, Wolfgang, or as he was known among his loved ones, Wolfie. Wolfie patted Clover on the head with a smile, and said, "Braver Hund!" He bent down and filled Clover's water dish, scratching the dog under his ears before walking away.

Clover and Wolfie lived near Hamburg, a German city near the North Sea. Wolfie's house was a cozy wooden cottage surrounded by wildflowers, daisies, and buttercups. Clover loved his home. Typically, his humans let him lie around in the back yard or in his own doghouse. Sometimes, especially when it was cold, he would get to come inside with Wolfie and sit by the fire or snuggle on the floor next to Wolfie's bed.

But today, Wolfie had no time for him. After giving him the water, the child had turned on his heels and run back into the house. Clover got over his momentary disappointment and sniffed the water. It smelled different: sweet like honey. Clover tilted his head, his tongue lolled out again. He bent down and started to drink. The water also tasted sweet. He lifted his head again, one eyebrow raised.

Ist dies ein Leckerli? Clover wondered, but it was too early for daily treats. He continued to lap it up. Maybe it was someone's birthday. Maybe it was *his* birthday, and no one had told him yet. A couple of hours later, he felt strange. Actually, he felt smarter and stronger than he had felt in years. His mind was clear and crisp. But this was quickly overpowered by a massive headache; it was so bad, he lowered his head between his massive paws. *What's happening to me?* He yelped and whimpered until the pain stopped late that night.

The next day, Clover was surprised to see an unfamiliar beagle lounging in the bushes near his doghouse.

"Hi, Clover," the beagle said in a friendly tone. Clover raised his head in confusion. He heard the greeting, but it was in another language—English—*and he understood.* He was delighted to see and hear another dog. Sometimes he got to go to the dog park, but it was rare.

"Clover, do you understand what I'm saying?" the beagle asked gently. "You've been given a gift from Robo, an amazing leader. Do you like it? Can you can understand a little more?"

Clover rose to his full height and nodded his head.

"Are you treated well?" The beagle cocked his head.

"Treated well?" Clover asked. "I'm loved. Wolfie and his family love me." He paused for a second. He had just spoken English for the first time.

"Well, you're a lucky dog: a lucky dog, indeed. I bet you'd like to make them proud. I bet you'd like to protect them better. I bet you'd even like to sleep in that house more often," the beagle said with a laugh, "instead of out here."

Clover looked at him suspiciously.

The beagle caught the scent of distrust. "How about you and me play some ball? Let's just get to know each other."

Over the next few weeks, Clover and the beagle, called Sniffer, kept talking—about dogs all over the world, and especially about the cruelties some dogs faced. Sniffer shared how Robo was going to make the world a better place for them *and* *humans*. Clover, who had not really thought about the world beyond his backyard, started to yearn for adventure and the chance to make a difference.

After a month, their conversations turned serious.

"Clover, could you make a sacrifice for a short time?" the beagle asked. "Robo wants you right now. He needs *you* right now."

Clover couldn't help but feel intrigued, but tried to hide his curiosity. "Seriously, Robo is a pretty stupid name," he said to the beagle.

The beagle laughed again. "Yeah, maybe, but Robo's tough and an amazing leader. It would be a shame for you to miss this…opportunity."

Sniffer encouraged Clover, saying that change would happen quickly, and that Clover could come back a better, stronger, smarter dog for Wolfie.

Clover made his decision.

On this morning, Wolfie, rubbing the sleep out of his eyes, walked into the kitchen. Clover—who had slept in the house— whined and scraped the door with his dull claws. Wolfie opened it. "Guten morgen," the child said in his sweet voice. Clover acted like he needed to go to the bathroom. The boy shook his head with a smile, and let him out into the front yard.

At first, Clover went to a corner of the yard to sniff. He saw the open road, and Sniffer waiting for him. He turned back to look at Wolfie, who was tapping his foot impatiently. Clover lifted his ears and started to whine. He didn't want to leave.

But then he started running down the road.

Wolfie quickly snapped from his daydream and sprinted after him. "Komm!" the child yelled, concern and worry in his voice.

"I'll come back! I promise!" Clover barked without looking back. The child tried to catch up, running down the dirt road after him. Eventually, Wolfie gave up, and collapsed to his knees, exhausted. But Clover kept running.

The last word he heard from Wolfie, crying, was "Please...."

࿐

Clover and Sniffer moved quickly toward the harbor. "You need to get on this boat—the black and white one," Sniffer told him. "I leave you here."

Clover walked slowly, unsure of this next leg of his journey.

Sniffer pushed him toward the freight dock. "You're going to do great, kid," he said, cheerily. "Now, go. A Pit Bull is waiting for you."

Clover waited for dark before climbing into the boat. As Sniffer promised, a muscular brown Pit Bull with a white chest was waiting for him, flanked by other dogs.

"Recruits, welcome!" the Pit Bull said, loudly. "Fall in line to join the best, most courageous pack in the world: Robo's army."

The new dogs, nervous and happy, shuffled next each other in a ragged line.

"My name, as my owner would say it, is 'Killa,'" the Pit Bull said. "But you can call me by my formal name, Killer," he said with a laugh. The dogs laughed nervously.

"You are strong. You are smart. Now it is time to see what you are truly made of," Killer said, pacing. "The water you drank has given you incredible power. You must learn how to use that power for Robo's mission. Are you with me?"

The dogs barked, the noise hidden from the humans by the boat's engines starting up.

"I said, ARE YOU WITH ME?"

This time, the dogs howled in unison, "Yes, SIR!"

Killer walked the line, and stopped in front of Clover.

"You certainly have some size on you," he said. Clover shyly looked down. "Look at yourself, Clover," Killer said. "You are magnificent, and yet, they treat you like a pet!"

Clover was taken aback. "I'm not a pet. A cat's a pet. A bird's a pet. I'm a family member!" he protested.

The Pit Bull scoffed. "Clover, you live in a back yard all day! You can't go with them when they go out and get food. When you get into the leftovers, they yell at you! They even say they 'own' you!"

Clover's eyes widened. "They only say that because they don't really understand what 'Alpha' means. That's all." He realized he didn't sound very convincing.

Killer snarled, "You're a stupid young dog! They have collars on you, marking you as their property! They put you on leashes and chains! You eat on the floor for crying out loud! That Wolfie, whom you love so much? Sometimes he forgets to even feed you. Does he apologize to you? No. And what does he feed you? Fresh meat? No, 'dog food' that tastes like dung."

Clover lowered his head, his ears down. Tears welled up in his eyes.

Killer realized he had gone too far. "Look, Clover. Robo has given you a chance to change that. You can return as their equal. You can truly be a family member, protecting them and loving them. We are going to make a difference in the way humans and dogs relate forever.

"Of course," Killer said slowly to all recruits, cringing now. "It is still your choice. We will dock at several ports in the coming weeks, and you are always free to go back to being a slave."

The dogs growled.

A Terrier approached the line with a laser punch gun. "This," the dog said, "will mark you as part of Robo's army. Are you brave enough?"

Killer turned over his paw, and the new recruits stared at the large pad. A symbol—a huge gear with a dog—had been burned into it.

Clover hesitated joining the line, and quietly cornered Killer.

"I'm happy to join," he said. "I truly am." With all the firmness he could muster, he said, "But I don't want anything, or anyone, to harm Wolfie."

Killer smiled, revealing torn gums and broken teeth. "Of course, kid."

Clover sighed. He missed Wolfie already. *I hope I'm doing the right thing.*

He got back into line, and winced slightly as the Terrier branded his paw.

CHAPTER 16

"I'M HEADED OFF TO MEET a dog named Raven. He might have some intel on your puppy," Copper said sincerely to Blue. "Rex has to return to base, being all fancy-dancy Special Forces."

"Well," Blue stood up, wincing in pain, "then I'm off to find this Raven, too." She stumbled and fell to the ground in agony. Nothing was broken, but all of her muscles were bruised and stiff.

"Not right now," Copper said sternly. "Right now, you need to rest."

"I can't now. I'm looking for my puppy." Blue stopped suddenly, realizing that was the first time she had claimed Max as her own. She shook her head. "I mean...a puppy."

Copper raised his eyebrow. "You sure he's really just *a* puppy?"

Blue lowered her head. *I hate caring*, she thought.

That night, Rex and Copper made sure Blue had plenty of food and water. She couldn't help but like them; dogs who feed you are friends for life. They howled with laughter as she shared how she tried to catch ducks in her mouth, and she captivated them with her tales of city life in Atlanta.

As the moon rose over the meadow, Rex taunted Copper. "Hey, Floppy Bunny, sing us some songs!" Copper could never turn down an invitation to sing. He lifted his head and howled out a few tunes, mostly about chasing squirrels and lost bones.

For the first time in a long while, Blue fell asleep feeling content and safe.

Rex was the first to rise the next morning. Blue heard him briefly talk to Copper, ending his conversation with a stiff salute and a "Yes, General." Copper returned the salute, before saying with a laugh, "That's Floppy Bunny to you." They both laughed before Rex bounded off.

Blue pulled herself to her feet with renewed strength. At first, she limped alongside Copper, but later she found she could run. Copper, sensing her anxiety, kept moving, leading them out of the meadows and toward the city of New Orleans.

It was springtime, so the air was thick with the smell of cherry blossoms and magnolias the size of white dinner plates. Spanish moss dripped from the trees, and the air was hot and humid, but bearable.

What was unbearable was the boredom.

Blue finally turned to Copper.

"Tell me more about SAD, 'General'," she said.

Copper narrowed his eyes and twitched one of his ears. "Well, I can tell you what we're facing."

Blue didn't answer, but nodded to tell him she was listening.

"Robo is a half-robot dog who has extraordinary intellectual and leadership skills," Copper said. "But you already knew that. He has also given his dogs enhanced strength, speed, intelligence. And he has assembled an army—a powerful army, mostly of dogs who have been hurt or neglected by the human race.

"We know from our intelligence that he is planning a major attack," Copper said, lowering his voice. "We don't know where yet, or how, but we see huge battalions of dogs all over the world moving into position. However, there might be a weakness in his plan," he said earnestly. "We believe some of these dogs might want to become part of the resistance—especially when they realize how insane Robo's plan truly is.

"At SAD, we believe humans and dogs were meant to live in harmony with each other. We have seen many humans with great compassion who treat dogs well. Our leader has experienced this first-hand. She survived cancer because of humans."

"Well, good luck," Blue said, sarcastically. "Because that sure has not been the track record of the humans I've known."

Copper grew quiet. "Well, that's too bad, Fuzzy Wuzzy."

Hours later, Copper stopped under a bridge spanning a murky river. He pulled out some rabbit meat to share with Blue, a parting gift from Rex. "We are on the way to see a dog with amazing powers," he said. "He's a Great Dane, like Robo. Get this—he can foretell the future."

Blue laughed, "That is so fake."

Copper nodded, "Yeah, some say he went crazy, and that's all it is. But even if Raven's crazy, he has spent most of his life around Robo, so he can tell us more about him, and maybe how to find him." Copper's voice dropped to a whisper. "My intelligence tells me that Raven foretold your arrival, and believes you might be the Chosen One."

He stopped, and took a deep breath. "So for once, please try to be nice."

Blue couldn't contain her laughter. "He's clearly crazy. He's got the wrong dog," she said. "I grew up in an alley. I play with potatoes. I run into trees. I don't even have a pack."

Copper countered, "You've been captured and changed by scientists. You've destroyed a speeding car. You captured the orb.

You have even stood up to coyotes, Dobermans, Rottweilers, and Bloodhounds. But hey, what do I know?"

Blue pondered what he said: *Ridiculous—so silly. SAD is so clearly wrong.*

Later that night, she found she couldn't shake a feeling of motivation—dare she say, hope—running through her veins.

After two more days of traveling, Copper came to a stop at the edge of a wasteland of ash, rotted trees, and thorny bushes. Mud from a recent spring storm made running difficult, so they slowed to a thick, gooey trot. After a few hours, Copper climbed through some burned logs and brambles, and halted.

An abandoned mansion stood before them, clearly glorious in its day. It was a massive Victorian house, with a large wrap-around porch, covered in overgrown wisteria and kudzu, a two-story turret, and a heavy slate roof. But it had been blackened by smoke and dirt and age, with many beams slowly falling in around the foundation.

Copper and Blue scrambled onto the porch, and carefully tapped on the carved front door. It fell to the ground, the wood around the hinges rotten.

They walked in cautiously.

"You go right, and I'll go left," Copper said, still looking around.

"Okay," said Blue, walking down the right passage. With every creak, her ears pricked up. She saw spider webs, dead rats, and old bones of animals long gone. Her back bristled. She sensed something ahead.

"Go away," an old, male dog growled from a dark hallway.

Blue quickly ducked into a small closet. She heard each of

his paw steps as he approached on the warped, wooden floor. She waited for the steps to pass. Instead, they stopped right in front of the door. She leaned back, getting ready to lunge. But as the door opened, Blue was too shocked to react quickly.

Before her was a light gray Great Dane with the strangest eyes she had ever seen. One eye was red with a white pupil; the left eye was white with a bright red pupil.

He slowly grinned, before muttering under his breath, "This is it. The prophecy."

Then very slowly, almost in a trance, she heard him recite:

*When good twists into bad, and bad grows into good
And flesh and steel become one,
Red will rule the world,
And all with prints will suffer.
But from deep waters, one will rise
With bones buried at her feet and gems for vision,
Who will show that rage does not justify revenge,
And tyranny and history do not own the future.
She, separated from the he, will dig, demand and restore
The chance for a new balance,*

He stopped abruptly.

"Oh," he said. "It's you, city mutt."

Blue was unnerved, and stumbled backwards. The bag around her neck swung as she moved, the leather cord strangely loosening and landing at Raven's feet.

He did not move to pick it up. Instead, he talked calmly to her.

"This orb, I know," he said, his voice halting on every word. "It has great powers."

Blue stared deeply into his other eye, which looked clouded and blind. As she got closer, she noticed an image of—how could it be?—a battle.

She shook her head in confusion, before seeing herself in his eye, fighting and wrestling with a robotic Great Dane. She was injured. Badly. She broke away, shaken by the reflection.

"Who are you?" she said, slowly. "*What* are you?"

He turned his massive head toward her. "You already know who I am, Blue."

Blue realized he was right. Somehow, she already knew she had found Raven.

Hearing the chatter, Copper staggered into the hall, his eyes dazed.

"Raven," he said, breathlessly. "I'm so glad we've found you. SAD needs your help with Robo."

Blue turned to Copper in disbelief. Surely, this insane, ancient dog was not going to be able to do anything against Robo.

Raven narrowed his eyes, staring blankly at Copper. "Oh? He's still alive?"

Copper remembered to show his respect for the old dog, and bowed deeply. Raven spoke slowly, his speech marred by pauses.

"The Eye of the Future shows that terrible things will happen to me if I come with you," Raven said with a low growl. "I have no desire to stop Robo from fulfilling his destiny."

He pushed the bag with the orb back to Blue. "Go," he said, his claws clicking on the floor.

Copper lowered his head, disappointed. "We've come all this way to talk to you. Raven, we really need you."

Raven was unmoved.

Copper said in desperation, "We can't do this without you."

Raven kept walking away. "Then you fail. So be it."

Copper turned away in frustration, and signaled Blue to follow him out of the mansion.

Blue, no closer to finding Max, looked at the old dog in disgust. "You should be ashamed," she yelled at him. "Copper has done nothing but talk about how great you are, but you're just an old, stupid dog who thinks of nothing but himself."

Raven turned toward her one more time. "Get out, Husky, who knows *oh so* much. "

She left, shaken and disoriented, but strangely glad to have the orb back in her possession, safely around her neck. They walked silently back through the burned grounds, defeated, with the mud sticking to their feet.

After washing up in the river, Copper looked at the sunset and said, "Let's rest here."

Blue didn't argue.

"Tell me more about Raven," she said softly.

Copper leaned in.

"Once upon a time," he said, then laughing. Blue rolled her eyes.

"Serious now," he said, his voice getting deep. "When Raven was a puppy, he was born from a weak mother. No brothers or sisters. He and his mother were doomed from the beginning."

Copper then told Blue how Raven's mom had been caught by humans who were dog fighters. She was called a bait dog—a female used to attract cruel stray males. Tethered by a chain, she couldn't get away, and was horribly abused by both dogs and humans. Of course, after the humans caught the fighting dogs they wanted, they killed her. Copper paused sadly. "In front of Raven."

Blue sighed. She had heard of such things, but had never known anyone in her circle that had actually been hurt in such a way.

"Raven was alone and young—only five months old," Copper continued. "But he managed to run away."

"After a couple of days, he was lucky to meet Bone, an Alpha dog who ran one of the world's largest city packs. In that pack, he met a lost puppy named Robo."

Blue's eyes widened.

"Raven and Robo became the best of friends as puppies, and on to adulthood. But for some reason, they had a falling out." Copper whistled softly. "A bad falling out. Robo attacked him, slashed him across the face, blinding him and leaving him to die.

"Although Raven lost his sight in the present, he gained an ancient power to see the past and the future. No one knew he had come from a line of seers—fragile in body, like his mother, but strong in spirit. As Raven gets older, he never knows where in time he is, which is why he often speaks slowly, sometimes drifting between dimensions.

"If you believe in that kind of stuff."

Blue was quiet, absorbing Copper's story.

"Anyway," Copper brightened. "He was adopted off the street by a nice woman who felt sorry for him. She brought him to that mansion, and for many years, he was lucky to be well cared for and well loved. Unfortunately, about two years ago, the house caught fire, and the old woman died from the smoke. Raven survived, but he has fallen on hard times as you can see, living on rats and donations of strangers who want to know the future as Raven 'sees' it."

Blue sat there. She didn't feel annoyed or skeptical now. Instead, she genuinely felt bad for Raven. After all, her mother was probably murdered by humans, as well, and she knew the pain of someone she loved being stolen from her...

She looked down sadly at her front paws. Copper noticed tears gathering in the corner of her aqua eyes.

"Well, looky here," he said. "We're in the middle of nowhere, and that means I am free...to sing. That means you, too!"

Blue looked at him in horror. "I don't sing," she stammered.

"You're kidding me, right?" Copper teased. "A Husky that doesn't sing? Why that's a *crime*. C'mon, it's not like it's that hard."

Blue muttered, "Well, I suppose the way you do it, that's true."

Copper laughed. "I will ignore that mean comment. Now, sing after me."

Robo is bad, bad, bad.

Blue rolled her eyes, but dutifully tilted toward the stars and sang,

Lego is bad, bad, bad.

"Nice job, Fuzzy Wuzzy. I'll tell Rex you like his nickname."

That's why we need SAD, SAD, SAD.

Blue muttered, "This is the worst song ever."

Copper growled, "Just sing, Husky." And Blue followed along.

His voice grew softer as he sang the last two lines:

So don't be Blue, Blue, Blue
Because I'm with you, you, you.

For a moment, they both looked at the stars and were happy.

Copper called Blue next to him. "Here," he said. "Stay close, and sleep well. We're going to have a long day tomorrow."

Blue snuggled against his large, lean body, curled up in a tight circle.

"Good night, Floppy Bunny."

"Good night, Fuzzy Wuzzy."

CHAPTER 17

WITHIN A YEAR, Robo had secret bases in every part of the world, so many that sometimes he lost count. The wind currents and his recruiters had spread the serum, making millions of dogs smarter and stronger. Even water supplies across the world contained the serum, thanks to the engineering of Dr. John Fox.

Many had flocked to join Robo, with tens of thousands already living in the homes of their humans, now the enemy.

All was going as planned. Except for that stupid Husky who still had the orb.

Right now, he needed to rally the brand-new troops here at his mountain headquarters, and around the world. With live feeds and cameras set up with the help of sympathetic, well-paid humans, Robo was ready to introduce himself to his legions of followers.

With a graceful leap, Robo landed on the platform. "Brothers and sisters!" he commanded. Silence descended in the auditorium. "I am Robo."

He grinned widely, his metallic teeth gleaming off the intense overhead lights. "What a sight I am," he said loudly, cutting the tension as some dogs, seeing him for the first time, were visibly shaken. And he was a sight to see, thanks to the evil Dexter—titanium legs, titanium canines, a robotic tail, a glowing red eye, and his pointed, scarred ears. He was too skinny, and appeared old.

The new dogs rumbled loudly on the floor, some now nervous, some irritated.

"Is this some kind of joke?" asked an angry Pug. "You don't look like a leader!"

The Pug continued, "What kind of cheap scare tactic is this? Just because you have robotic parts doesn't mean you can lead this revolution."

Robo's mechanical eye focused on the Pug, scanning his size and other stats.

He made eye contact and winked at the first row. He laughed, and said, "Perhaps this will be more impressive."

He dimmed the lights before filling the monitors with hundreds of other bases in different countries, all run by dogs.

"No one has to be here," he said in a low, steady voice. "You have all been given intelligence and strength, and you have also been given freedom. No longer do you need to be loyal to anyone merely because it is instinct. For the first time, you can be loyal because you have found something worth being loyal to."

Robo cleared his throat, his voice rising louder, and more powerful.

"You might be confused or scared tonight," he said. "But I am here to tell you it is time to take back our ancient rights. For thousands of years, people have abused us, forced us to fight, locked us in cages, and done horrible things." He paused and turned his head toward the crowd.

"I have a proposition. I have the power—*we* have the power—to change our destiny. We do not need to be tied to that of humans, no longer will we be chained against our will!"

The dogs howled in agreement; even the Pug leapt up and down.

Robo motioned for Sabu to silence the crowd, and got on the scaffold to be lowered to the auditorium floor. The cameras followed him at close range for his majestic walk among the dogs.

Most parted to make a path for him, but others leaned in, trying to capture his attention. Robo stopped before a Pit Bull. "What's your story, brother?" The Pit Bull, with a limp and a scarred face, said loudly, "I had an owner—a real nice guy—but he was a gambler. When things weren't going so well, he lost a bet, and I was the prize." The Pit Bull looked down. "This new owner. He liked to watch dog fights and make money off them. He hit me and forced me to do terrible things to other dogs. It was kill or be killed."

Robo leaned in to him, placing his natural paw gently on top of that of the Pit Bull. He looked at the Pit Bull eye-to-eye, before turning away and raising his voice to the others.

"Look at this. Not even his 'owner' cared that much about him," Robo said. "How many of us have been sold, and resold, or worse, abandoned. How many of us have seen this happen to our own pups?"

The dogs growled and howled their agreement and anger.

Robo moved on through the crowd.

"What about you, big guy," Robo gently asked a Saint Bernard. "What's your story?"

The dog looked confused and shy, glancing down at his furry paws. "My name ist Clover," he said in a shaky voice and a thick accent.

"My human hasn't really done anything wrong to me,"

Clover said almost apologetically. "He has fed me and given me water, and when I have been good, I have slept next to his bed."

Robo contained his disappointment, but said slowly, "So, Clover—our German friend, from your accent—you got to sleep in a bed, if you were 'good.'" Robo laughed.

Clover now looked terrified. Robo nuzzled him good naturedly, and said loudly, "Well, we're just glad you're here," before he climbed back on his scaffold.

"Look," he said, addressing the crowd again, "I understand that life with the humans might seem great to you, when it's all you have known. But I'm offering you a much better life, a life of the ruler instead of the servant." He paused. "Brothers and sisters, join me!"

Robo turned to his pack and bellowed to them, "Help these recruits prepare for their new lives." The pack immediately moved into the crowd, helping them find sleeping dens and food, as well as training them for their new jobs and roles.

In the confusion, Clover had stopped trembling. He suddenly felt sad as he thought about his youngling's small bedroom, filled with homemade comforters and crayon drawings, hardly big enough for both the boy and the Saint Bernard.

"Come with me, recruit," Savage barked at Clover, who hurriedly followed.

Meanwhile, Robo summoned Unknown, Splat, and Snow, a white wolf, to the control room. As he waited for their arrival, Robo peered at the largest monitor, tracking Blue. Today, she was traveling with a Bloodhound. Blue looked tired and skinny, covered in mud.

"Perfect," he murmured, as he heard the steel doors open.

Unknown and Splat, whose face wound was still healing, arrived first, followed by Snow.

Robo cleared his throat. "I have a new opportunity for you to get things right," he said to Unknown and Splat. "I want you to bring me Blue, unharmed." He swiped the screen, bringing up Blue's location. "Take what you need from the pack to get the job done right. If you fail again, at least get her to this meadow," The monitor showed the map coordinates.

They hesitated.

"Well, GO. NOW!" he barked, and they scurried through the doors.

૨૬

With the room still, he turned to Snow. She was beautiful and graceful, with sharp, perfect white teeth.

"We need more troops," he said quietly to her. "However, these troops will be a different breed."

She stared at him, her head cocked, failing to understand.

"Our friend John Fox has been able to recruit more scientists and engineers for our cause," he said. "With their help, we have created a new prototype of dog."

Robo swiped the screen again, and Snow stared at the new image before her. She realized she was looking at a new, sleeker version of Robo: a true hybrid of robot and dog. Snow looked back at him in admiration. "That is spectacular," she said with appreciation.

He laughed. "Well, it's been hard to get every dog to... cooperate."

She nodded. "Always the way with progress."

"Snow, I need you to go to this meadow and be the Alpha of a pack we will establish. If this Husky and the Bloodhound arrive, you will offer them shelter, and when they are comfortable, you will help Unknown and Splat capture her, and bring her to me."

He looked at her, and she suddenly felt shy.

"Do this for me," he said, gently, "and there will be a place by my side waiting for you. Now go," he said, with a quick nod of his head. "Do not fail me."

Snow bowed quickly. "Yes, Robo."

PART 3

But from deep waters, one will rise
With bones buried at her feet and gems for vision,
Who will show that rage does not justify revenge,

CHAPTER 18

COPPER TURNED TO BLUE. "Let's get some sleep here. You look half-dead, and I think I can count all your ribs."

Blue then realized how sore and hungry she was.

Copper dug a large hole into the black, ashy ground providing a dry inner shell. He jumped in, curled up, and called Blue to do the same. Ever since she was a pup, she'd never felt comfortable sleeping when other dogs slept, with her mom always telling her to sleep in shifts in times of danger to protect everyone. But now, she never felt so happy just to close her eyes and sleep.

A few hours later, though, Blue woke up to a sharp smack to her back. She felt a dog lift her by the scruff and throw her to the ground. Her eyes open, fully alert, Blue recovered and pinned the attacker to the ground. Her eyes adjusted and recognized Unknown now squirming under her. Unknown no longer looked like the fragile weakling she was before—she looked strangely powerful.

She was. With ease, Unknown kicked Blue off, and tackled her. "You're coming with us!" Unknown growled.

Blue squirmed away and backed into a rock. She felt Copper's flank. Turning toward him, she saw that he was cornered by Splat, who had a new scar across his cheek. She growled, her fur standing on-end, bristling.

Unknown rose on her hind legs in an attempt to knock Blue out.

"Cease!"

Blue turned and saw Raven in the shadows. He stood there staring blankly into the distance. "I am done with all this violence, especially on my territory." He bared his teeth. Unknown's eyes widened in momentary confusion. "How are you still alive?" she asked, growling and charging Raven. Raven rolled his eyes and deliberately raised his paw as she approached, smacking her hard in the chest.

Unknown got up, her head down, body heaving. Splat looked at her in shock, and looked at Raven with a snarl. Copper sprang in front of him and growled, "Keep walking, Hairy Chest!" Splat cocked his head in confusion, and ran, with Unknown close behind.

Blue and Copper chased after them, Raven joining in.

Copper howled, "Raven, thank you. Thank you for your help. Live long, brother."

Raven, however, didn't slow down, shouting, "I'm coming with you."

No one had time to argue, and Raven had no time to explain.

Unknown and Splat took advantage of their lead, and ran as fast as they could—staying just ahead.

※

When Unknown and Splat disappeared from sight, the three found themselves in a meadow with soft grass, and a stream that fed into a small pond with cattails. Plump rabbits nibbled on the grass. "Evidently, no wolves or coyotes," Raven observed, sniffing in their direction.

Blue and Copper were still dirty, cold, and tired. Copper suggested they build a den of leaves and sticks. Blue pushed leaves into a heap against a large log near the pond, and hollowed out a place for them to sleep. Exhausted, the three nestled together to rest. Raven curled up in one corner, facing the wall, Copper in another corner, but turned toward Blue. Blue took the remaining space. As they huddled in the dark, Copper spoke first.

"So why did you come, Raven?"

"Boredom," Raven replied in his halting voice.

Blue rolled her eyes. "Wow, aren't you miserable?" she muttered to herself.

Raven's eye twitched in irritation. "Shut up, city mutt."

Blue was taken aback by this. To her, Raven was old, wise, and a little bit crazy, not someone who would insult others easily. She held her tongue.

"I'll take the first watch," Copper said. "You get some sleep."

Blue, her feelings slightly hurt by Raven, burrowed deeper into leaves and drifted off.

⁂

With a full moon above, Raven woke up in the middle of the night, thirsty.

He got up slowly, his muscles sore and his joints hurt. As always, his eyes were bothering him. The lure of water from the stream he had seen earlier pulled him out of the den. Tracking the scent of the pond animals, he found the stream and drank deeply. In the stillness of the night, he thought about his life—the dogs he loved and valued, the human he treasured. In his measured, logical way, Raven thought about his death. After all, death visits all: the poor, the rich, the masses, and the magnificent. Despite all his scars and close calls, Raven could not help but fight the idea of his own demise. "Why does it have to end like this?" he muttered to himself.

Suddenly, he sensed another dog's presence. In the moonlight, Raven detected the outline of a beautiful creature—a white wolf with vivid blue eyes. He crouched down to watch her as she drank deeply from the stream. She appeared to be talking to herself in the night, which he didn't find odd as it was his regular habit. He stayed hidden until she left, and then he went back to the den.

At first light, Blue woke with a start. Her coat was a tangled mess; gaunt and weary, she looked pitiful. When she looked up out of the den, she instantly saw a white wolf looking at her in clear disgust.

The wolf's nose wrinkled, as she sniffed the entrance. She growled with contempt, "Don't you dogs believe in cleaning yourselves?"

Blue, Copper, and Raven froze, each calculating her next move. The wolf, realizing this, changed her tone.

"I'm sorry, what a terrible hostess I'm being," she said softly, her long, luxurious tail flirting with Copper. "I'm Snow, Alpha of my pack. I'd like to offer you some peace and quiet to pull yourselves back together for the rest of your journey. But if you could stay a little while, I could definitely use your help. We're trying to strengthen our pack—we've heard rumors of trouble coming. We need a lot of paws on deck right now."

The three looked at each other. Blue, feeling weak and looking at her thin, tired companions, said, "I think we can do that."

"I'm delighted," Snow said. "Follow me."

By the end of the day, Blue was tucked into a new, clean, den. But, for some reason, she had trouble sleeping. The constant noise from the pack annoyed her and kept her on edge. She finally decided she would sleep outside. Quietly, she got up and jogged outside toward the bushes outside the camp. It seemed the farther away from camp she got, the better she felt. She was cold, but welcomed the feeling. Finally, she found a patch of moist grass, and slowly curled up and closed her eyes.

⁂

Copper woke up first. He had expected the other dogs to wake up sooner, but realized that the others might not be on his sleeping routine since they have constant training from 5:00 a.m. to 9 p.m.

Unlike Blue's desire to get away from the noise of the pack, Copper was up before dawn for a different reason. He had a meeting with Rey, a brilliant Chihuahua. They were both SAD generals supporting Alpha Gem, their leader. He bounded out of the clearing while it was still dark out. He walked a distance away from the camp, sat down, and adjusted his earpiece to SAD's secret frequency. Mindlessly, he hummed the song he and Blue had sung a couple nights ago.

Suddenly he heard a voice.

"Hello Copper," said a high-pitched voice.

Copper lowered his voice.

"Hey, Rey."

A slow chuckle echoed through the microphone. "What's wrong with you Copper? I can already tell something's wrong."

Copper only sighed in response.

The chuckle stopped. "You didn't take care of that dog, did you?"

"No, I did not," Copper said. "I think it's pretty clear that she's not with Robo's army."

"How can you be so sure?" Rey asked, irritated. "You're willing to put the entire operation of SAD at risk for one mutt?"

Copper stayed silent, his eyes drooped. "I don't feel like this is the appropriate action for this dog, I think there is something special about her. Raven sees something in her too. He said she could be the one prophesized."

Rey quickly snapped, "Raven is crazy. Have you gone soft in the head?"

Copper shook his head as if Rey would see.

"The prophecy? I can't believe you're giving that any hope. Who believes in prophecies when we have real armies to face?"

Copper studied his paws silently, and Rey realized through the silence he had been harsh.

"Look, I trust your judgment, but if you're wrong, this will be brought before the Alpha Gem. Again, I warn you, you're putting us all at risk."

Copper slowly nodded, and murmured "I understand."

The earpiece went silent, and Copper closed his eyes. He was fond of Blue, and now he needed to seriously rethink whether his discision to trust her was a good move. "What am I going to do?"

Meanwhile, Blue had returned to Snow's camp. The dogs were working together happily, building their dens. Everyone seemed remarkably healthy.

After living life on the streets, Blue couldn't help but be cynical. "This is too perfect," she thought.

But she decided to move past it—for now.

CHAPTER 19

BLUE'S SUSPICIONS ONLY GOT WORSE over the next couple of weeks. First of all, the pile of prey never seemed to be touched unless Blue or her companions ate first. Next, when she went to sleep, there always seemed to be flashing bluish lights in the dens. However, since she was still healing, she didn't have the energy to snoop around to see who they were—or what they were—and she didn't want to cause trouble.

They always smiled and worked long days. "Too good to be true," Blue thought, thinking about all the dogs she knew who spent their days napping.

But there was still…something. She took the time to carefully bury her leather bag with the orb in a secret place because the place didn't feel right. Even Copper started to act nervous and twitchy around her, and he wouldn't even hum anymore. One night she found him watching over her while she slept.

Then it happened.

Blue was out getting some exercise and fresh air one night, when she heard voices. She crept into a bush.

Two of the camp dogs were talking. "Must kill you," one of them said.

"Please no—I'm just looking for my mother," one of two yearlings whined.

"You crossed territory."

"There's no markings, no scent, no boundaries," the second

yearling whined.

Blue crouched low, and slowly crawled closer to the voices.

She gasped. A young, female Black Lab and a strong, young male wolf were just feet away from her. The Black Lab looked strangely like Destiny, with the same white patch on her ear. How could that be?

Blue's eyes widened in shock, but she sprang forward when she saw the camp dog's front paw rise to strike the two yearlings. As Blue emerged from the bushes to shield them, the black Lab saw her and started to howl, "Blue! Blue!"

Blue felt the rake of claws on her stomach. Despite the deep scratch, she stood tall and proud. The dogs slashed again; this time the blow was to Blue's forehead. Blood dripped into her eye, but she felt no pain. Instead, she was filled with two emotions: anger toward these dogs, and excitement that Destiny was alive and here with her!

Blue prepared to defend herself and rescue the yearlings, but one of the camp dogs began to plead with her.

"H-help m-me," he said. "Robo. Robo is shutting me down." The dog turned to the other one and said, "We have failed."

Huh? thought Blue.

She watched in shock as clumps of fur started falling from the dogs' coats. The one who had pleaded for help disintegrated into a pile of fur and metal. Blue realized they must have been half dogs and half robots.

The other dog started to collapse in front of her, crumbling into the ground. He looked at her with remorse in his eyes, whispering, "H-help." His voice was hoarse and ruff. He collapsed to the ground and died.

Blue barely had time to absorb what had happened when she felt six paws smash her against the ground. She struggled under the three new camp dogs that had pinned her down. As she lashed out at them, she tore their fur, exposing robotic parts. She watched in frustration as the puppies were also pinned by Snow's pack.

The wolf puppy gritted his teeth. He stretched out his claws and slashed one of the dogs' throats, but the robot didn't seem phased. The yearlings were overwhelmed and beaten.

At the same time, Blue saw Copper being dragged by two more dogs. Raven wasn't anywhere to be seen.

Snow, the beautiful white wolf, slowly walked toward them. It was hard to see her at first in the dark of the night. At first, the only way Blue knew it was Snow was because of her pale blue eyes, standing out against her white fur and the blackness of an incoming storm.

Snow stepped toward Blue and sniffed her chest. "Where is it?" Snow growled. "Give it to me! Give it to me NOW."

Blue refused to answer, pushing Snow's snout out of her chest. Snow seemed strangely distracted, and Blue heard her muttering under her breath, "Robo won't be pleased. He won't be pleased at all."

Snow looked nervously above her at a bright light suddenly blinding them. At first, Blue couldn't see through its brilliance, but as it drew closer, she recognized it as the spotlight of a helicopter, which was slowly descending.

Once landed, the helicopter's door slid open.

Out walked Robo.

CHAPTER 20

BLUE STEPPED BACK IN HORROR. This was the dog she had seen leading the killing armies in Raven's mystical eye!

Robo's mere size caused the other dogs to retreat and bow, ears drawn back. His right front leg and right hind leg were monstrosities of technology made of titanium and green fluid. His right ear was now merely rods and circuitry with a current of energy flashing like a halo over his skull. And his eye—his right eye was spellbinding. Made of three parts, the eye almost looked like a goggle with metal, mesh straps holding it place. The lens had a constant red glow. And finally, there was the cruel titanium rod that held it all together, screwed directly into Robo's skull.

As he slowly stepped off the helicopter, there was no sound in the meadow except for the loud, powerful swoosh of his smooth hydraulic parts. He scanned his surroundings before walking directly over to Blue. He sniffed her before demanding in an icy snarl, "Where is it?"

Upon her silence, he turned to Snow, back hunched and head low, and repeated the question. "Where is it, Snow?"

Snow rolled over in submission as she spoke meekly, "She's hidden it, and I can't find it."

Blue watched his metal paw slash through one of Snow's perfectly formed ears with the precision of a sword. The beautiful white wolf was no longer perfect.

He turned back to Blue, still held down by three other dogs.

Robo looked down at his bloodied robotic paw and wiped it on his broad chest. He narrowed his eyes and turned to Blue, "I'm so sorry, Blue. This is not how I wanted to meet you. But this is simply business."

Blue challenged this claim. "You just slashed another dog for *business*," she snarled. "I don't think you know the meaning of the word."

Robo's eye darkened and he smirked. "Wow, not even scared. I'm impressed, Blue."

He turned away from her and walked toward Copper. Robo curled his lips, "General, you know, I've been keeping a close eye on you."

Copper rolled his eyes. "If you intend to kill us, you can always skip the chit-chat. You know, let's just be all *business*."

Robo chuckled, "I have no intention of that, but thanks for the idea. You always did talk too much anyway, Copper."

He turned toward Destiny, her eyes wide with fear. She shrunk away from him.

"Well, hello there. Dusty, isn't it?" Robo asked, and Destiny instinctively stuttered, "Destiny." Robo smiled warmly. "Oh, my mistake," He lifted his head high above her. "For some reason, I thought Claw had killed you. He should have, so why are you still alive?" Robo snarled viciously.

Destiny yelped in terror and put her paws over her face, as if to make him disappear. Robo turned toward the young wolf. "And of course, Duncan. I'm not surprised to see *you* here, next to all the traitors. If my paw didn't already have blood on it," he looked over at Snow, who had slunk away, "I would kill you right here.

"Okay, now that we've had our introductions," he said, "Blue, where's the orb?"

Blue cocked her head. "Why do you care?"

Robo said, "I need it to do...certain things."

Blue shook her head and laughed. "Sorry, I'm gonna pass on helping you with the end of the world, and all that," she said in a defiant tone.

Robo shook his head. "I'd kill you quickly if you didn't know where the orb was."

Blue sneered, "Then it's a good thing I know where the orb is."

Robo shook his head. "You naïve dog. You have no idea what you're getting yourself into."

"Oh yeah, I'm pretty sure I do," Blue said simply.

Robo sat down, his natural eyebrow raised. Narrowing his eye, he spoke softly, "You know Blue, I can search around in your head to find out where you put it. I have the technology, I can force you to tell me where the orb is."

Blue sneered. "I'd like to see you try."

"In fact, I think I can do even better," Robo said. "Maybe we should have our scientists implant fake memories into that very teeny, tiny brain of yours, and cause you to murder everyone you love."

Now Blue was listening.

"My Dog! Can you just tell us your super evil plan?" Copper shouted sarcastically, interrupting the argument. Blue and Robo both looked at him.

Robo sighed and walked over to Copper, who was crouched

low in a fighting stance. Robo reached toward Copper and yanked out a small earpiece, hidden in his long ears. "Classic SAD." He smashed the earpiece into the ground, small sparks flying.

"You know, Blue. You've been working for the wrong side; Copper here was supposed to kill you," he laughed.

"You're lying," she said, but there was insecurity in her voice.

"Oh no, my little alley mutt. I'm afraid I'm not."

Robo rose to his feet, and turned to the robot dogs.

"Put the General in the helicopter, he'll be necessary. Meanwhile, Blue and I are going to take a little walk to find the orb." The robotic dogs nodded, forced Copper to his shaky feet, and pushed him towards the helicopter. Copper lowered his head and gave a low, menacing growl. Blue turned, worried he was going to try to fight his captors.

Instead, he lifted his head and, with his Alabama twang, started to sing.

Robo, you're just like a Lego.
I can take you apart
And you don't have a heart
And you're acting like a great big FAAAART.

Copper drew out the last word with a classic Bloodhound howl.

The robot dogs looked stunned. Even Robo was knocked off guard.

Then there is Blue,
She's a Debbie Downer too,
But you must admit,
She's a lot prettier than yooooooooou.

"C'mon everyone, sing along!" Copper bellowed, now throwing his paw around a robot dog like an old friend.

Robo's soldiers, confused and disoriented, finally gave in, their last remaining memories of being real dogs kicking in. Some sang about squirrels, others, lullabies from their puppyhood.

Robo looked in horror at this howling, singing, out-of-tune choir.

Blue felt a cold nose prod her during the distraction. She jerked her head around and saw Raven. He had the bag with the orb around his neck, and Destiny and Duncan at his side. Quickly, he slipped the bag over Blue's neck, taking advantage of the distraction. They slowly backed away from the helicopter. Once Copper noticed them gone, he leapt over his captors and ran toward his friends.

"Get them!" Robo yelled.

☙

Blue led their escape. A burst of adrenaline ensured their getaway. She didn't dare stop. Robot dogs snapped at their heels, and she could still feel their breath on her tail. Her heart pounded.

Suddenly, Blue dug her paws into the dirt, wincing in pain, trying to halt.

A giant gorge was ahead with a waterfall roaring down the side of the cliff. Blue turned, panting. The robot dogs were gaining on them.

She saw rocks piercing out the edge of the gorge, and she howled to the others, "Down the rocks!"

"Not so fast!" Robo slid in front of them, blocking the only escape for Copper and Blue. The two pups were able to slip past him, and quickly jumped down the rocks, disappearing before the robotic dogs could reach them.

Robo's natural eye flamed with hatred. He screamed at Blue and Copper, "You're not going anywhere!"

A laser fired from his metallic shoulder, and Robo aimed it at Copper.

Raven had been hiding in the underbrush, and leapt forward, smashing into Robo's side. The laser still fired, tearing into the rocky ground, causing it to crack under Blue and Copper.

They both fell into the rapids below.

Water filled Blue's mouth, and she struggled to breathe. The current was too strong for her to swim. She flailed about desperately, hoping her claws would find tree limbs or anything to keep her from drowning. Because it was still night, she couldn't even be sure which way was up.

Finally, she broke the surface. Her vision was still blurry, but she managed to make out Copper's bobbing head in the moonlight.

Blue realized he was trying to swim towards her. It was too late. The waterfall consumed them both, and Blue felt her stomach drop. The water took her under, but this time she didn't fight; she was too exhausted.

She closed her eyes, defeated. Suddenly, she felt jaws grab onto her scruff and pull her back to the surface. Blue opened her eyes only to see Copper being swept away.

Blue whimpered, "We have to get him!" But a cold voice answered, "We can't," Blue realized Raven was her rescuer. He had a small gash in his shoulder and large claw marks on his chest.

"Copper is gone." Raven answered, his eyes dull and blank. "Let him return to the Open Meadow, as we all must do when our time is done."

Blue felt her eyes burn, and hung her head between her paws. "No. No. NO!" she whimpered.

She lay down on the beach, her fur heavy with water. Too many dogs had left her. She no longer had the energy or will-power to go on. She closed her eyes, thinking about Copper, the sweet Bloodhound who had made her laugh, that had made her sing, that had believed in her.

The grief was too much.

"Um, Blue?" Destiny whispered, interrupting her thoughts. "Look up."

Blue turned back toward the waterfall and saw Robo standing at the side of the cliff. He started to jump from rock to rock, with his army following close behind. His robotic eye was smashed, oozing red liquid that burned the fur around it.

Blue lowered her head, shivering. She closed her eyes. She didn't care. Let Robo capture her. Why should she make friends, just to lose them? Love is pain and she had had enough.

Raven twitched nervously, waiting for Blue. Finally, he muttered, "Oh for Dog's sake, Blue," and started to forcibly drag her to her feet. Blue snarled, nipping at him. He ignored her, saying, "Stop thinking just about yourself."

Finally, he pushed her, along with the others, into a thicket of sweet smelling blackberries. It was perfect—the thorns protected them from an easy attack, and the berries hid their scent from the rapidly approaching dogs.

They watched as Robo roared, "Go go go!"

The panicked robot dogs ran past the thicket, intent on pleasing their leader. When they had safely passed, Blue crawled out.

"They'll be back soon," Blue announced, and ran back to the river. She had noticed some dead fish on the bank earlier, and now dragged them around the trail to throw off the robot dogs. She hoped to buy enough time to give Destiny and Duncan a chance to escape.

Blue returned to the others. "Run away, as far as you can," she said sternly.

"But why? We want to help," Destiny whined.

"Yeah, why can't we help?" growled Duncan.

Blue said to Duncan, "I know we haven't known each other for long, but I'm counting on you to protect Destiny. To help her survive."

Duncan replied, "Destiny already knows how to do that, remember? She's been on her own for a long time now without me or you."

Blue winced.

"I was left in an old coat in a brick wall. I couldn't find you," she said, hurt. "I looked for you and Max, but couldn't find either one of you. I didn't know what to do. I was almost dead until Vince found me."

Blue looked confused.

"Vince," Destiny continued, "It was his coat. He was homeless, like me, and he saved my life."

Another human who wanted to do the right thing.

"Just do as I ask," Blue said firmly to both puppies.

Duncan growled his displeasure, but finally nodded. "Fine, whatever. Though, I would love to get my paws on that stupid, old mutt, Robo"

The thought of losing Destiny twice broke Blue's heart. But Destiny would be safer with Duncan. Blue still had to try to find Max.

Blue nuzzled Destiny. "I'm so glad you are alive. I'm praying your brother is, too."

Destiny nuzzled Blue back, with tears in her eyes. "I just found you. This is so unfair. I've been looking for you forever," she cried. "I need to give you this." Destiny lowered her head and something that had been previously hidden in her coat of fur slid off her neck and onto Blue's neck.

It was a necklace that held a stone with a husky's image burned into it.

"Destiny, where did you get this?" Blue asked.

Destiny studied her paws shyly. "I stole it."

"Stealing?" Blue laughed. "What a great alley dog! I'm proud of you."

Destiny brightened with the praise.

"I want you to have it—it was meant for you!"

Blue shifted uncomfortably and looked at the necklace. She softly said, "I'll treasure it."

Destiny started to cry again. "I believe in you, Blue."

One last time, Blue licked away Destiny's tears. Destiny breathed deeply.

They heard more barking outside the thicket. "No more talking," Blue warned in a low voice.

They waited until the barking faded away. Then, Raven and Blue said their final goodbyes to Duncan and Destiny, who started running, leaving the fields, the woods, and the river behind.

Raven and Blue went the other direction. The rocky ground under their paws transformed into rich dirt, which slowly turned into sand covered with driftwood and shells.

Blue stopped to survey her surroundings. They were on a beach by a still body of warm, salt water. When Blue waded into the greenish-blue water, she could see straight down to her paws.

"Where are we?" she asked to Raven.

Raven said, "It's the Gulf Coast, city mutt."

"Are we going the right way?" Blue asked with concern.

"The right way does not necessarily mean where we're meant to be," he said crisply. "We are where we are meant to be."

They continued to run on the sand.

"You know, stealing is bad…" Raven spoke up.

Blue sighed. "Oh, please, you've been a dog in tough times before. We both know that stuff isn't simply handed to us. Besides, I'll probably give the necklace away anyway. It's like a huge choking hazard and I don't want to worry about it."

Raven shook his head. "Do you think she gave you a necklace because she thought you would choke on it?"

Blue laughed. "Why else would she give it to me? I've

already abandoned her twice."

Raven sighed. "She loves you in a way that you can't possibly understand," he said. "You're so blind sometimes, Blue."

Blue grew silent.

⁂

Hours later, there was no freshwater and no shade. Just the constant smell of saltwater and fish. Even Raven's patience was running low. With the midday sun blazing down, they both were tired and thirsty. Their mouths started to crack, their noses and eyes burned from the salt. All Blue could think about was the great shade trees and the fresh water fountains in the parks of Atlanta.

Suddenly, Blue saw a dark figure rise up from the waves of heat.

"Oh no," she rasped, taking a step back. "Is that one of Robo's dogs?"

Raven shook his head slowly. "No, it's something else."

The figure came closer, and Blue realized it was a thin brown dog with bright purple eyes. *Purple eyes? Surely this must be a mirage*, she thought.

With tail wagging, the brown dog bounded over to them. "Wow, I never thought I'd see dogs out this far. You two look pitiful."

She noticed that Blue had her ears back, suspicious and distrustful.

"Relax, little Sheila," she said. "I was just about to say hello." She bowed with a flourish. "My name is Ash. Dingo at your service."

Blue did not want to like this dog.

Raven stepped forward. "We would like somewhere to rest please. We've had a very long day."

Ash nodded. "You look pretty knackered. If you can hang in there just a bit longer, old chap, I'll take you back to the pack."

Blue glared at Raven. "What are you doing?" she snarled quietly.

Raven answered, "Not dying."

CHAPTER 21

THE FUR AROUND ROBO'S ROBOTIC EYE was still smoking. He pushed past his deputies. Unknown walked toward him, her head down and small ears limp.

"Ro-robo?"

Robo quickly turned around, and gripped his jaws around her throat to subdue her. She could feel his teeth, and whimpered with fear.

"Shut up!" Robo snarled, letting go of Unknown. "You can't do anything right. None of you 'full' dogs can. I can't count on any of you anymore—not you, not that stupid Snow, none of you. All of that intelligence is wasted."

He turned to his deputies, lifting his paw toward his pack, and bellowed, "Do what these worthless full-ones have failed to do."

The metal from his deputies was shining in the morning sunlight streaming through the windows. They answered with a crisp, "Yes, Robo."

Robo pulled up his tracker, and found that Blue and Raven had collapsed in the sand.

"They're already half-dead," he said, mildly pleased. Addressing his commander, he said, "Finish the job and get that orb."

The commander turned back to the deputies. "Let's go."

As they filed out, Robo decided to walk the halls of his headquarters. There were no puppies, just the sound of dogs barking and growling, the clank of metal limbs on the floors and stairs, commands being uttered, and the constant hum of the ventilation system.

Suddenly, he saw a human running. Robo was startled—and alarmed. Quickly, he chased and tackled the human, pinning him to the ground.

Robo snarled at him, "Where are you going?"

The human, staring at the teeth inches from his face, tried to use his hands as protection. His wire rim glasses were bent, and Robo's claw had left a cut on his cheek with a few drops of blood now splattered on his white lab coat.

Robo felt the presence of another dog. He turned his head to see Clover.

"Clover, why is this human here, out of its area?"

Clover gulped air, but answered honestly. "He tried to escape. He started to run, and I was chasing him to put him back in the lab."

Robo rolled his eyes. "Well do it! Now!"

Clover began to drag the engineer by his leg back to the lab.

Robo returned to the control room, enjoying the still solace and soothing blue light from his monitors.

Sabu interrupted his thoughts.

"What now?"

"The scientists have developed a new formula," he said. "But we need a test subject."

Sabu glanced at a monitor for a long time, which showed the Saint Bernard dragging the scientist back with gentle force.

"Not that one," Robo said. "I have a much better choice—the yellow Labrador. Max."

CHAPTER 22

BLUE OPENED HER EYES SLOWLY. She felt soft sand on her paws, and looked around to see that she was in a small, rocky den. She was sore. Bruises were everywhere. *Bruises? Where did I get these?*

Oh. The waterfall. Suddenly the memories came flooding back, and a pang of sadness for Copper swept over her. She tried to lift herself up.

She failed, right as she heard a sweet, tender voice.

"Don't get up. You are too hurt and hungry."

Blue felt a rough tongue licking her ears, a comforting gesture she remembered from puppyhood. Blue knew it was the right thing just to lie down. But where was she? She moaned.

"Have some water," Ash said, pushing a leaf filled with water. Blue drank it in a few rapid slurps. She tried to get up, but her legs felt like jelly. Still, she stiffly walked out of the den. Her eyes burned in the light. Slowly, she walked with Ash from den to den.

"Where's Raven?" she finally asked in frustration.

"I think he's the last of your concerns," Ash said. Seeing Blue's expression, she quickly replied, "Follow me."

They arrived at a secluded den in a cave, where a Chow Chow watched Raven, giving him a sniff here and there. Her nose suddenly rose in Blue's direction. "What do you want, city dog?" she snarled.

"He's my friend," Blue snarled in return, angered by the Chow Chow's attitude. She walked over to Raven, following the sound of his shallow breathing.

"Wake up," Blue commanded. Raven opened his strange, red-and-white eyes.

"I have heard of such ancient powers, but never witnessed them," Ash said. The Chow Chow nodded in agreement. "Who are you two exactly?"

Blue opened her mouth to speak, but was cut off.

"No one," Raven answered.

The Chow Chow cocked her head. "It seems we have some stubborn—"

A loud howl of pain echoed through the cave, and all four quickly stepped outside. An injured dog, covered in blood, limped toward them. Another dog rushed up to help. The injured dog's eyes where filled with fear.

"The-they c-c-came o-out of n-n-n-nowhe-where." He could hardly speak from blood loss and shock.

Ash sniffed, "He's severely injured. Come with me."

The Chow Chow nudged the injured dog forward toward the den.

"I'm getting tired of this! Half of our dogs have been attacked," a dog with deep scars on his flank and neck howled.

"QUIET!" the Chow Chow commanded. The howlers obeyed. "I'll send a patrol out to take care of the problem."

Blue quietly moved closer to the large Chow Chow. "What problem?" she whispered.

"The dogs with metal—the half-breeds," the Chow Chow said, looking Blue over for the first time with true interest. "But since you're no one, I suppose it doesn't matter."

"Blue. My name is Blue," she growled. She said something she had never said before: "I would like to help."

The Chow Chow viewed her suspiciously. "My name is Jenny. I'm the leader of this pack." She shook out her great reddish mane, looking more like a small lion than a big dog. "I will take you up on your offer. Go get some rest and eat some food, city mutt."

Hours later, with fur brushed and belly filled, Blue sat next to Jenny, looking over the pack from a ridge.

Jenny leaned in to Blue. "In the past few weeks, we have been under constant attack from these strange dogs. They seem to be looking for something or..." Jenny looked at her suspiciously again, "someone. I need a patrol that can learn more about these half-breeds. And I need you to lead it."

"Why me?" Blue immediately regretted offering to help. "I just got here, why trust me?"

Jenny narrowed her eyes. "I want to see what you can do," she muttered.

Blue knew she was lying. She looked down at Jenny's injured pack, watching them limping and counting their scars. She realized that Jenny had no other options, but was too proud to admit it. Blue breathed deeply. "All right. Let's do this."

Jenny nodded, and turned toward her pack below.

"My brothers and sisters," she started, but the pack was in disarray, driven crazy with news of more losses and injuries.

Blue rose up next to her. "Quiet," she barked. "QUIET."

She barked so loudly that she could feel her voice echo off the rocks over the wild dogs.

The dogs stopped in their tracks and looked at Blue in amazement.

"I will lead the patrol tonight," Blue said. "I have a history with these robots. I know their weaknesses. Together, we will bring these attacks to an end." For a brief moment, Copper flashed through her mind. She paused. "I'm so sorry for your losses." She meant it. Jenny studied her paws in shame.

She gritted her teeth, "Any questions?"

The dogs were too shocked to say anything more.

"Good," Blue said, and followed Jenny from the ridge.

Blue and Jenny then set up a patrol of five dogs.

"Let's go," Blue commanded, looking back at her soldiers. They walked silently onto the empty beach. After a few hours, one of the dogs signaled for them to stop.

"We're getting close to their base."

The patrol hunkered close to the ground. Blue could smell their fear. They could smell her rage.

"There it is," another dog said.

She looked toward a steel base that rose from the beach like a metal mountain. Robot dogs were screaming commands at each other.

"YOU GET IT," one of the dogs howled at another.

"NO, YOU GET IT!" the other screamed.

They morphed into a rolling ball of anger, snapping and snarling. No one bothered to stop the fight. The other dogs had glazed expressions, acting more like zombies than dogs. Finally, the fight ended when one of the dogs ripped off the other's robotic hind leg.

"How do we do this?" Blue asked, more to herself than to

the patrol.

"We could surround them," Ash suggested. Ash had joined the patrol to help with any wounds.

"We should attack them right now," another dog said, his chest puffing up at the thought.

"That is a stupid idea," said a third.

"You're stupid."

"No, YOU'RE stupid."

Blue couldn't comprehend what she was witnessing. Dogs on patrol against a deadly enemy, bickering like pups. Bickering loud enough to be heard.

"Shut up," Blue said quietly. They didn't listen.

"Shut up!!!" Blue snarled with a quiet intensity that stopped the dogs immediately. They stared at Blue.

In that moment, Blue heard a rustle behind the marsh grass. A wind blew the grass aside, revealing a robot dog with one eye. The dog was tiny. It was a pup, she realized.

One of the dogs, with hair raised, snarled at it. "Back off, half-breed."

Blue stared at the puppy, panic rising in her throat. For a moment, she thought she was looking at Max.

"Blue," Ash said quietly.

Blue looked again and realized it looked nothing like Max. It had dark long gray fur, looking almost identical to Robo with its metallic legs and an artificial eye.

"Don't touch it," Ash continued.

The pup whined, crawled toward the patrol, and rolled to the ground, his belly revealed.

"Is this some kind of joke?" the other dog growled.

The puppy tried to talk. "Help me..." He barely had the strength to finish. "These dogs did this to me—the mean Great Dane."

Ash, breaking her own advice, walked to the pup and sniffed him all over.

"He's telling the truth," she said, her purple eyes suddenly brimming with tears.

Blue stared in horror.

There were seams where steel had been fused into his bones, stained with blood. There were claw marks deep in his back from where he had been held down. He had scars in his stomach, and even claw marks in the metal. Blue's anger intesified.

"Blue?" Ash asked, worried.

Blue gently picked the hurt pup up by the scruff. The pup let a small whine.

"Hold on for a second," Blue said, before finding the puppy a safe place to hide while the team moved forward.

The patrol team watched the base throughout the night, and as Blue followed their movements, she became convinced that they could infiltrate the base. The plan was to distract the dogs and disable their power supply.

Blue explained to two of the dogs how to disable the base's power source.

While they snuck into the base, Blue quietly pinned the robot guards until they passed out. Then, at the right time, she signaled the two dogs to advance to the power supply. She and the other patrol members moved deeper and deeper into the base, taking more guards down. The two dogs found and crippled the power plant, throwing metal scrap into the generator,

Blue's first mission was a success.

Despite scratches and bruises, Blue didn't feel any pain. She was driven by the need to stop these robot dogs and avenge their cruelty to the puppy. She limped back to the patrol, which were still surprised that they had dismantled the base and won.

"Let's go." Picking up the puppy, Blue gently tossed him on her back. "Hang on."

As they re-entered their territory, the pack was gathered together. SAD agents had already detected that the base's power was down and alerted the pack. The pack knew that Blue and the patrol must have been victorious.

"You will always be remembered in this pack!" Jenny howled, her tail wagging in joy and her eyes full of relief.

Blue suddenly remembered her quiet, injured passenger. She reached behind her scruff and pulled the robot pup down.

All the dogs gasped.

"How dare you bring that thing back here?" Jenny growled, she stepped forward inches from Blue's nose.

"He's just a pup, and he can barely even raise his head. He's in so much pain. Please, invite him into your pack," Blue asked. "Do this. Do this for me."

The pup whimpered in pain, and started to cry.

"They cornered me. They cornered all of us—to use for new tests," he cried. "I lost my mommy and my daddy. My brothers and sisters. Everyone." He collapsed next to Blue, burying his head under his metallic paws.

Jenny looked at the pup in horror and shock. It was so helpless, so awful.

Ash stepped forward. "I will care for the pup," she said. "I give him passage into our pack."

"Fine," Jenny growled. "Blue, let Ash care for your wounds. But I must ask you to leave once you are fit enough to travel." Jenny eyed Ash.

"We thank you for helping us, for teaching us how to fight back," Jenny said firmly. "But I strongly suspect that there will be payback, and they will be looking for you. We will escort you safely to the edge of our territory, but then you are on your own."

Blue nodded. "I understand."

⁂

Robo turned off the monitor in disgust.

His base was crippled—a loss among hundreds of wins. Even though his deputies told him not to worry, he knew better. This Husky knew how to fight his army. Even worse, this Husky knew how to win.

CHAPTER 23

BLUE FELT GREAT. She had not been this healthy for a very long time. Her fur was sleek, and her wounds were healed. Blue was now the strongest, fastest, and smartest dog at the beach.

The half-robot puppy seemed to be doing well in Jenny's pack, fitting in with new friends. He was named Rover, and Ash became his adoptive mom, caring for his cuts, and cleaning up the infections around the metal parts.

Blue loved to watch Ash with Rover. She was constantly making him little treats of lizard and bird meats to build up his strength. As Blue watched the two together, heads touching, she grieved for little Max and Destiny, and wished she still had both cuddled next to her in her den.

It was almost time for Blue move on. She realized that, in order to defeat Robo and be reunited with Max and Destiny, she would have to leave this peaceful paradise.

Raven was also doing well physically, although he seemed to be more anxious and agitated. One night, Blue stumbled into his den and was stunned to find him crying. He refused to tell her why, only muttering, "We cannot escape our fate."

❦

On this day, Raven took her out to the beach, acting cold and quiet as he always did. He stopped and hesitated, then nodded to no one in particular. He turned toward Blue, pacing.

"In order to defeat Robo, I will have to train you," he said quietly. He turned and walked away.

He had already told Jenny—who was somewhat relieved to hear that they would be leaving for a few days. After brief good-byes, she watched Raven and Blue walk toward the ocean. She had been grateful for their help, but she knew they also brought danger. It would be better for her pack when they left for good.

Blue tilted her head as they walked to the dunes again. *I've never seen Raven as a fighter...*

Raven lifted his head toward the sky, impatiently. "Hurry up, Blue. I want to begin our training tomorrow, and I want to be near the waves." Raven gave her a sharp glare. His eyes still scared her at times.

"Are you listening to me, Blue?" Raven growled. "We don't have much time."

Blue nodded. Although she was in much better shape, the heat was taking its toll, making it hard for her to keep up.

"I must train you to fight unfairly, because if you don't, the world will use you, distort you, and kill you," Raven said firmly.

Blue chuckled, breaking the awkward tension. Raven looked insulted, but Blue ignored him.

"Do you know anything about me, Raven?" she growled. "I was raised on the streets and stole food from kids to survive."

Raven shook his head and walked on ahead of her. They walked silently, keeping a distance between them until they saw the sand and waves. Both of them were tired.

Raven suddenly whipped around, curling his lips in fake anger and snarled.

"Attack me," he said.

Blue was taken aback at this request. She was thirsty and exhausted, but never declined a fight if she knew she could easily win. She sprang toward the weak, old dog.

Surprisingly, Raven dodged out of the way, sending her rolling through the sand. As she flew past him, Raven bit hard into her tail and pulled her off her feet. Blue whipped around. She attempted to lock onto his throat with her teeth, but he was too fast. He slipped around her and used his back leg to hit her in the hip, knocking her off balance. Her annoyance turned into hot anger. She tried to push her feet into the sand so she couldn't fall. But her feet only kicked the sand up, creating a cloud. She couldn't see. Blue tried to blindly spring at Raven, but he grabbed her throat and slid her effortlessly across the sand again. Now, she was not only badly beaten, but also exhausted. Her throat was dry and her eyes hurt. She lay there, gasping for breath.

Raven shook his head. "You really are just a punk city mutt," he said. "You can't get angry. If you let anger take over, you get clumsy and waste energy. You're still thinking about yourself. See, real leaders don't lose their temper in battle because they have to be there for their team, their army, their families."

Blue quickly got up and looked at him, still not happy about losing.

"You cheated!" she snarled.

"I cheated? What, are you a puppy? And here I thought you were the Chosen One." Raven raised his eyebrow and turned around, flicking her nose with his tail.

Blue narrowed her eyes and snarled, "Don't turn your back on me!"

Raven turned halfway and snorted. "What you need to learn,

Blue, is to control your anger. Really think about being the *servant* instead of the *master* of your destiny," Raven said. "If you even have a destiny to fulfill, which is questionable at this point."

Blue felt her eyes well up at the insult. "Why are you always so mean?" she asked, trying to keep the hurt out of her voice. "What do you know about destiny? Maybe you're just a fake."

Raven shook his head and continued to walk away. The heat waves blurred him into nothing.

Blue sat there alone. At first, she felt sorry for herself. She had been through so much. No one cared about her, and those who did were either dead or missing. She seemed to do nothing but fight recently. Blue started to cry.

But after she stopped, Blue realized that Raven was right; she had led a selfish life. She hadn't cared about anyone else until Robo's cruelty forced her into new situations with new friends. She thought about the poor little stray abandoned by his humans she had threatened and mocked for his belief that they would return. She felt ashamed.

She was the one who had been mean; the one who had been bad for no other reason than it made her feel powerful.

Blue grew still.

She decided she would use her new, barely tested powers, for good. Finally, she fell asleep on the beach, at peace.

The next day, Raven stared down at the Husky, who was curled up in the marsh grass. *Such a silly dog. How does the future see this mutt as special?*

Blue opened one eye, seeing the Great Dane above her.

"Your breath stinks," she said.

Raven laughed. "Not as much as your fur does. You smell

like a dead bird."

Raven backed up into a fighting position: head down, feet braced. "Let's try again." He was poised five feet away from her. With a curled lip, he baited her. "Attack me!"

Blue got up, lowered her head and paced around him, studying his posture. She felt her limbs stretch and tingle and she realized this was the sign. *My powers are on.* She felt lighter, like she could run forever. Raven studied her movements. Blue sprang toward him, baring her teeth. This time, she was not going to let Raven walk away. She felt energy pump through her body, and this time, Raven was barely quick enough to block her. He just managed to spring out of the way, using his back leg to trip her. She fell to the ground, and slowly got up shaking the sand off her head. She spat out sand, frustrated and angry.

Raven trotted up to her.

"You don't know how to control your powers. Until you do, stop relying on them, Blue," he snarled. "Your anger is still blocking your good sense."

It was another long day. She slept alone on the beach again.

The next morning, Raven stood above her again. He didn't even say good morning. She dutifully trudged after him. He walked up onto a steep, sandy hill. She followed. Raven sat on the edge, and shared his fresh water with Blue, who gulped it down gratefully. He sighed, looked at her, and then looked down on the beach, marsh weeds swaying in the wind.

"Why are you here, Blue?" Raven asked, turning toward her and, for once, meeting her gaze.

Blue was taken aback at this question. "Why do you want to know?"

Raven sighed, "You need a reason to fight against Robo. You just can't fight out of anger all the time."

Blue sat still for a moment, studying the marsh down below.

"Obviously, I'm fighting for Max and Destiny, " she said. But then she grew quiet. Why did she have to face Robo? Freeing Max? Avenging Copper? She'd never cared about other dogs before, certainly not enough to risk her own life. What was it about this battle that made her feel she could not walk away?

The vision. Again, she saw the destruction—the lives lost, the fire, and Robo behind it all. Everything—dogs, humans— everyone suffered. Even Blue, selfish, city mutt Blue, felt like the scientists had given *her* the power to fight this evil.

"I don't want dogs and humans to be ripped apart," she said. "I'm still working through my feelings on this, but I think, although some dogs have bad owners, the good ones don't deserve death, which is what Robo has planned for them. Most people love their dogs, and, sadly, even their cats. It's already a messed-up world as it is. If anyone knows that, I do. I don't want Robo, or anyone else, to make it even worse." She lowered her voice, and looked down the beach. "Secretly, I think I just want everything to be perfect, and it is so frustrating when it can't be. I guess I want to fix it so no one else has to," her voice growing more intense "And then I was given the same powers. I mean, how weird is that? So, maybe it really was meant to be. Which, I know, sounds crazy when it comes from me, a 'city mutt' with no family left. But maybe you're right. Maybe I am the *one* who has to bring him down."

Blue stopped talking, and looked over at Raven. "Did you even listen to anything I said?"

Silence.

"I know how you feel about dogs and their 'owners,'" Blue said slowly, and Raven looked at her without emotion. "I know you must have loved your human, Raven."

Raven looked down, studying his paws, remembering his human with her curly tendrils of gray hair, kind blue eyes, and her wide-brimmed straw hat that she wore in the gardens around their home.

"I also know you must have loved your mother," Blue said at a whisper, her own mother flashing in her mind. Raven stared at her in understanding, as if he had looked into her past and saw her grief.

Raven cleared his throat, shook off the memories, and bounded down the cliff.

"Come on, Blue."

Blue followed him. They walked along the coast for about an hour. When they finally stopped, Blue was even more confused. A boulder stood in front of them.

Raven walked by it, and finally spoke, "I want you to move this rock."

Blue cocked her head to the side. "What?"

Raven closed his eyes in frustration. "You're a terrible soldier. You don't ever do what others ask you to do."

"Well, you didn't exactly ask," Blue said under her breath. She could feel Raven glaring at her.

"Okay, okay, hold your leash," Blue muttered, as she walked toward the rock and forced all of her weight against it.

Nothing. Blue felt her strength drain, and she quickly gave up.

"It's hard to do something on your own, remember?" Raven

said. To Blue, it seemed like he was mocking her.

Raven softened his tone. "Come, get up. Try again, this time I'll help you."

Blue rose frustrated. "Fiiiiinnnnnneeeee."

She pushed all her weight into the boulder again, which remained unchanged until Raven finally helped her. She felt the rock shift, and she realized that, with Raven's help, they had moved the rock. Blue sat down, breathing heavily.

"There is power in working together, Blue."

Blue sighed, "I guess there is."

"Sweet dreams, Blue. Even Chosen Ones need their rest."

Blue laughed. "Not much to being the Chosen One when there's only two of you," she said.

"Pack members stick together," Raven responded. "Even when the pack consists of only two."

He dug a shallow hole in the sand, and curled up into it. With a nod of his nose, he signaled Blue to do the same next to him.

Blue was a little irritated. "Could we please not sleep on the beach?"

Raven closed his eyes. "I'm taking you somewhere tomorrow, and I don't want to waste time in the morning."

Blue rolled into her spot, and closed her eyes. Despite her annoyance, she fell instantly asleep.

Blue felt wind rush across her face; her wings were spread wide across the sky. Her beak was bright yellow and reflected the rays of sunlight. She was a falcon, soaring above high rises of Atlanta, feeling powerful and free. As she swooped in and out between the tall buildings, she noticed dozems of dead and injured birds who had fallen to the sidewalk, their necks broken. What was happening? Why were they dying?

Then she looked toward the skyscrapers again. Their walls looked like mirrors, the reflective glass giving a deadly illusion of open space. The birds had made an error in judgement, and had flown directly into the buildings. They had believed they were headed toward freedom, but instead they had flown to their deaths.

She glided to the sidewalk, full of sorrow. As she looked at her reflection in the polished glass, however, she wasn't a falcon any more. She was a Husky, tall and powerful, with glowing aqua eyes. Around her neck was the glowing orb. Blue picked up a brick in her mouth and threw it at the building. The walls shook and then cracked, shards of glass plummeting to the ground. Reflected in each shard, she saw the red eye of Robo. Blue tried to dodge the pieces, but she could feel them piercing her, blood splattering against her white fur.

Blue heard the wings of thousands above her. She looked up to see flocks of birds flying above her. This time, they didn't fly toward the deceptive buildings, but toward blue sky. They knew the truth now, and Robo couldn't hurt them anymore.

CHAPTER 24

BLUE WOKE UP IN A START, and looked around for Raven, who rose to his feet and twitched his tail for her to follow him. They walked for about an hour in silence until Blue couldn't take it anymore.

"Where are we going?" Blue moaned. "Please don't waste my time again with more silly exercises."

Raven paused, and then turned to face Blue. "I grow tired, Blue. You always feel you know everything, and you don't ever consider other dogs'—friends or foe—ideas or plans."

Blue narrowed her eyes. "How much do I need to understand here? Robo's the bad guy and I'm the good girl. Done. Got it. Move on."

Raven laughed and rolled his eyes. "But why is Robo bad, Blue?"

"Why is that even important?" she growled. "Robo is an old dog. Not a dog you can change, but one you must stop."

Raven turned back toward her in frustration. "You realize Robo was my best friend, right?" He turned away from her and stared up at the sky. "Learning a dog's history can expose his strengths and weaknesses. I remember him before all this. I was loyal to him, and thought he was loyal to me. I trusted him. I loved him as a pack leader, and I loved him as my best friend. In the end, he used that weakness against me. Now, you need to understand who he is, if you want to win against him."

Blue stared at Raven. "So are you helping me because you want revenge?"

Raven bitterly turned away. "Not at all. I still care for him," he said sadly, "But I care more for the dogs that are suffering under his rule. He's gone crazy."

Blue looked at him, confused. "This is not your battle. You could just walk away."

"I tried that, but for whatever reason, I just couldn't. Plus, free dogs have nothing to lose. No one knows that better than you." He straightened up to his full height, both eyes burning with passion. "Sometimes you need to know when to submit to the fate you have been handed."

He started walking again. Blue followed, though annoyed at being lectured to again.

"You know, Robo was loved by his family. Not his pack—his *family*," Raven continued. "His mother had died, and he would have died too, if not for Becca and her parents. His true love was a little girl. Her true love was an abandoned gray puppy."

Blue was genuinely surprised. "He loved a human?"

Raven bounded into an abandoned beach shack, easily shoving the screen door open.

"Yes. As a matter of fact, he used to come here with her on vacation, and they would play on the beach. They were some of the happiest memories he ever had."

He motioned for Blue to follow. She looked in. It was clear no one had been here in years. There were fragments of broken furniture and cans left over from the damage of the last hurricane. Raven went over to a broken bed, and pulled out a scrap of construction paper. On it, a crayon drawing could still be seen: Stick figures of a little girl and a little gray puppy. Hearts and butterflies surrounded them both.

Raven looked up at her. "You've said it yourself, most humans are not terrible. My mother was once given a giant piece of raw fish from a nice lady who saw her on the street. She was starving, but even so, she brought it back and shared it with me. We were on our last legs, and that was a rare good night—a good memory among a lot of bad ones.

"Of course, no human is perfect. Heck—no dog is perfect either. We all have messed up, but seeking out the goodness that exists in all of us is what makes things better. Sometimes, you need the darkness to recognize the light."

Raven stared at the ground in sadness. "Robo hasn't seen light in many years." He then lifted his eyes toward her. "Neither have you, and I'm worried you will end up like him, lost in a dark cloud. Being worried about anything at my age is an unfamiliar feeling for me."

Raven walked out of the building and headed back toward the beach. They finally reached a dock, and Blue breathed in the fresh ocean air.

"Isn't it pretty?" Blue asked, her eyes bright.

Raven nodded, standing at the very edge of the dock. "Hey Blue, look, you can see fish! Why don't you come and see?" Raven sounded so unnaturally happy, she jumped at the chance to join him.

Blue walked toward the edge of the dock, but as she looked down, she didn't see anything except a strange ripple in the ocean below.

"There are no fish h-"

Suddenly, she felt Raven push her into the water, and the waves were dragging her under. Her breath was knocked out of her, and she fought to break the surface. Blue heard Raven above her, barking at her.

"If you fight, you'll die. Give in to a force stronger than you."

Blue didn't listen. *Raven is trying to kill me. I thought he was legit! Why would I think Robo's friend was my friend? Why didn't I realize he was a traitor all along!*

She felt pain from this betrayal, but kept fighting against the current. She was going to get out of this ocean and then she was going to *kill* Raven. She kept paddling against the current, but wasn't able to pull out of it. She was getting tired. This went on for several minutes before she gave up. She couldn't see Raven anymore. This is how it was all going to end. Everything she had done, everyone she had known was fading away. Her mother. Destiny and Max. Buddy. Copper. Blue couldn't breathe any more under the water. She stopped fighting. Her body relaxed, and she let the tide pull her under. Blue expected death to come.

❧

Okay, maybe I went too far, Raven thought. This was the problem with being a seer—everyone thinks you know how everything is going to turn out. But sometimes, you can really blow it. He bit his lip nervously.

He stared out at the rip tide, hoping that she had heeded him. Nothing.

Despair started to sink in. He had killed her. He thought he was training her, but he had killed the last hope that the world had. Raven frantically scanned the beach, as he ran off the dock and along the water's edge.

Finally, he saw where the riptide released its passengers. He caught a glimpse of a flash of white fur being pushed along the surface.

Blue!

Raven's heart skipped a beat. Blue drifted toward land, her head bobbing low in the waves. The water grew shallow and still. With one last push, a small wave deposited her body on the wet sand. Raven quickly ran to her to see if she was alive.

She was too tired to kill him as planned. Instead, Blue just looked up at him, spitting out water. "I hate you so much right now."

Raven, relieved, started to laugh and lick her with true joy, bounding around the white mop of wet fur. When she realized his joy was genuine, she forgave him.

Later, with her fur almost dried out, Raven explained to Blue his "dumbest idea yet." He had intentionally thrown her into a riptide— riptides tend to be dangerous only if you fight them. If you relax, letting the current take you where it wants to go, it's pretty easy to end up on shore, safe and sound and no worse for wear.

"In other words," Raven told her, "if you let fate carry you, and don't fight it all the time, you'll end up exactly where you need to be."

Of course, he said solemnly, he should have never tried to teach the lesson at the risk of Blue drowning.

"I'm so sorry," he said, quietly. Blue knew he meant it.

"Well, as you said, none of us—even those of us who can *supposedly* tell the future—are perfect."

After digging for crabs, and letting Raven groom her long white and black hair, Blue asked, "Now, can we go back?"

Raven nodded, and they headed back toward Jenny's pack.

CHAPTER 25

BLUE'S MUSCLES WERE ACHING and her eyes were heavy by the time they finally reached Jenny's pack. She stopped to eat a couple of lizards the pack had for a late night dinner, and went straight to bed.

"Psssst." A voice echoed in the dark, early morning hours.

Blue shifted uncomfortably.

"Pssssssst," the sharp voice hissed.

Blue opened one eye and saw Raven. "Will you never leave me alone?" she asked, half-joking.

Raven wasn't playing. "Training."

Blue slowly raised her head and yawned. "Why so early?"

She dutifully followed Raven with no more protests, keeping quiet as to not wake the other pack members. She was rather surprised when she saw Jenny sitting on a rocky ledge.

Jenny was staring deeply at the moon with a puzzled expression on her face. Her concentration broke when she saw the other two.

"Oh hello, Raven and Blue."

Raven dipped his head in respect. "Hello Jenny," he said quietly. "What are you doing up this early?"

Jenny frowned. "Same question for you."

Raven dipped his head again, and quickly responded, "More training."

Jenny nodded her approval. She looked back at the moon.

"I'm deciding whether this strange blood moon is a bad omen."

Blue cocked her head to the side, and was taken aback by the reddish moon still visible in the morning sky.

"Well, you keep doing what you're doing," Raven muttered, turning to walk out of camp.

Blue followed behind, and soon they were padding along on soft marsh grass.

"Okay, Blue, let's go. Pretend I'm one of Robo's guards," Raven said, taking his fighting stance once again.

Blue narrowed her eyes and said, "Got it."

No longer a beginner, Blue slowly circled him, studying his body and looking for weaknesses. This time, she realized his back legs weren't firmly braced.

Raven was sick of waiting, and lunged toward her, jaws snapping. Blue quickly veered out of the way. Raven regained his balance and lunged again. This time, Blue swirled around and clamped her jaws onto his back leg, tripping him. He was back on his feet within seconds.

Blue narrowed her eyes in anger. She was almost out of breath, and she knew that if she didn't have a strategy and didn't get her anger under control, she was going to lose again. She closed her eyes momentarily to compose herself; and then noticed a weakness. Raven was tall, even for a Great Dane, but also thin. If she slid correctly, she could possibly go under him and attack him from underneath. If he was a foe, it could be deadly: a direct bite to the stomach.

Blue smirked and ran toward him. Just as Raven prepared to strike, she slid to the wet ground, using the mud and sand to help propel her under him. It worked perfectly, and she gave him a small nip on the stomach.

There was only one problem: she continued to slide past him and into the rocky bank.

"Blue!" Raven's panicked voice echoed in her ears.

Blue attempted to get up—but no luck.

"Oh, thank Dog!" Raven yelped. "Don't try to move," he said.

Blue groaned, and again tried to rise to her feet.

"Here we go again," Raven said. "You just ignored everything I said."

He saw there was no stopping her. After a few false starts, it was clear that Blue was going to be okay. They started the journey back to the pack in silence.

Raven spent most of the walk back thinking about whether Blue—who kept making progress, but not fast enough—really could be the Chosen One. Blue, still aching and unnerved from her most recent injury, spent the time hoping she was not.

Once back with the pack, Blue rested from her head wound. Ash visited her often, chatting with her, and encouraging Blue to stop fretting and to relax.

"Healing the soul," she said, warmly, "is just as important as healing the body."

After some time, Jenny gathered Raven and Blue together. "Enough training. You need to meet your destiny—and it's not staying with us," she said, simply. "It's time to leave."

Jenny assigned a scout to walk with them to the edge of the pack's territory.

The morning they left, Blue and Raven said their goodbyes to Ash and Rover. Rover licked them both with enthusiasm, his wounds healed and his heart firmly tied to his new mother. Jenny and the rest of her pack waited for them on the rocky marshland. They gave the travelers a formal salute, howling in unison in thanks for a much-needed victory.

Blue looked at the sky. It was a clear, sunny morning. She hoped it meant good fortune.

CHAPTER 26

BLUE AND RAVEN HAD BEEN WALKING with the scout for what seemed forever. Slowly, the terrain started to change again—the ground became soft mud, and long rows of gnarled oaks were draped in Spanish moss and half submerged in swamps.

Blue smelled fear from the scout.

"I'm sorry I have to leave you here. All I can tell you is to watch out for this territory's pack. Black Tail, the pack leader, doesn't like other dogs in his territory."

The scout walked away silently after a gentle nuzzle with Blue and Raven.

Blue stared at Raven. His eyes remained locked forward, barely acknowledging the scout's departure. He walked straight toward the swamp, disappearing into the fog.

Blue cocked her head in confusion. Yes, Raven always was a little mysterious, but now he was just acting weird, and she was worried. She followed him slowly. The greenish water hid their scent. They moved across the swamp, their paws sinking into thick plants and bubbling mud. They often found themselves chest-deep in muck.

Blue kept alert, but also tried to engage Raven in a conversation, or at least an occasional laugh. He would not respond. Instead, he continued to lead in silence.

Soon, they heard the rustle of something moving through the swamp.

Did Raven hear it, too? She couldn't tell as he continued to move straight forward.

As night fell, the swamp became pitch black. Still a city dog at heart, Blue could never get used to this dark stillness; she could barely see her own paws, let alone Raven. She bit hard on Raven's tail so she wouldn't get lost. It worked until Raven accidentally bumped into a tree, and Blue lost her grip on his tail. She fumbled around trying to find it again, but she felt nothing. She clamored in the darkness. No matter what she did, she couldn't adjust to the blackness. To make matters worse, she was chin-deep in mud, and still sinking. Clawing in the muck, finally she found a solid patch of dark, green grass, and pulled herself onto dry land.

"Raven!" she howled in the darkness.

She felt a hit to her shoulder. A deep snarling roared in her ear. Blue could just make out a Newfoundland standing over her, with long black fur and large paws. Blue's shoulder throbbed, and she feared for her life.

He spoke to some dogs behind him. "Two dogs found here today. They're both actually alive."

As soon as Blue's eyes adjusted to the dog's presence, she noticed that Raven was being held down, too. Raven looked as calm as ever, staring blankly into the darkness. Blue tried to spring forward to help him, but the guards pushed her back into the muddy water with a splash. She climbed back to shore, spitting muddy water.

Blue decided to try to find some common ground. "I'm looking to fight Robo, the Great Dane."

The dogs laughed, only their teeth visible in the night.

The Newfoundland gave a chuckle, but his eyes snapped to attention. Slowly, his smile gave way to a frown. "Robo? That's the stupidest name ever. Let's try this again—tell us exactly why you are here, and if we like your answer," he looked around at his pack, "we'll let you go."

"Look, I'm telling the truth. We have no issue with you. Let us go on our way," Blue responded. "We heard you were a tough leader, Black Tail, but not a murderous one."

The dogs laughed harder.

"We don't have to murder fellow dogs, sister," Black Tail said. "We leave that to the crocs."

Suddenly, a soft, raspy laugh shut the dogs up. Raven looked at Black Tail, a strange and *scary* look to his eyes.

"Oh please, Black Tail. By the end of this conversation, no one will be worried about the crocs."

The dogs laughed again, but this time, there was a nervous edge. Black Tail sneered at Raven, "What do you know, old dog?"

Raven stared up at him. "What do you know, pup?"

Black Tail's laughter was gone. He commanded his pack—a mix of labs, golden retrievers, and Irish setters—to take Blue and Raven as prisoners. Just as the dogs moved toward them, spotlights hovered over the swamp, coming from half-dozen helicopters. The noise startled the frogs and crickets into silence.

"Blue, we know you're there," a voice said through a loud-speaker. "Give us the orb and we won't hurt you or those waterlogged beavers who call themselves dogs."

Blue felt her blood turn cold and her eyes grow wide. Raven stared up at the light, a glint of fear flashed in his eyes.

Black Tail snarled at the insult, but quickly organized his

troops. "Run! Encircle the craft when they try to land!"

Barking directions to each other, the water dogs started swimming and running through the swamp, forming a tight formation as the robot dogs dropped from the helicopters on ropes. Black Tail quickly had several dogs on the front line, and others crawling silently toward its flanks.

The robot dogs formed a line, waiting for commands. The captain, armed with his own robotic eye, then used bright, bluish LED spotlights to sweep across the swamp. The robot dogs plunging forward with precision, a wall of steel, sharp teeth, and claws.

The water dogs watched in horror as the robots swung machine guns from their shoulders into firing position, while another platoon of robot dogs cornered Black Tail, trapping him in a net.

"Retreat!" he yelped to his pack, most of whom were able to silently disappear into the swamp.

Blue tried to turn back as well, but three robotic dogs dug their claws into her back, shoving her into the soft mud and pinning her. Focusing her powers, she easily bucked them off as crocodiles began to glide near them. But she didn't see the fourth robotic dog. As he lunged forward, she tried to jump away, but he was fast. He sunk his teeth into her neck and held on as Blue dragged him through the muck.

Suddenly, a croc reared up in front of Blue. She quickly kicked it in the snout, plunging the croc back under water. It reappeared, and snapped at the dog still gripping Blue's neck. This time, the croc succeeded, biting through the dog's tail. The dog let go of Blue, howling in pain.

Blue continued to battle the robots. She heard the yelps of water dogs as the robotic dogs hunted them down. She tried to run again, but this time, a band of robot dogs surrounded her. Blue looked around wildly for Raven. No sign. Instead, she heard a low, deep voice reverberate through the swamp.

"How many dogs have to die because of you, Blue?"

A single red eye appeared in the darkness, shining brightly. It got closer, the eerie light casting shadows on Robo. He walked toward Blue, and sat down in front of her. As the guards held her, he slowly bent down and took the orb out of the leather bag around her neck.

"Don't you dare touch that, Robo," Blue threatened. "Or else—"

Robo's eye flashed with anger. "Or else, what, Blue? Will you use your 'special' powers?" he snarled, his nose now within inches from her own. "The only reason you have those powers is because of ME!"

She didn't dare meet his deadly gaze.

"So, Blue, where is Raven?" Robo asked.

Blue felt her blood turn cold. "He's dead. A croc ate him."

Robo laughed, "For a city mutt, you're a terrible liar."

Blue curled her lips. "Well, you would know."

"You're pathetic," Robo cleared his throat. "I'm going to ask again. Where. Is. Raven?"

Blue shrugged. "Lego. I. Don't. Know."

"You remind me of myself when I was young and stubborn," he said, with a faint smile. "But insulting me won't get you anywhere." Robo looked at the guards who had Blue pinned down. "Put her in a cage for now. We need to find Raven."

The guards nodded. "Yes sir."

Blue was forced to her feet, and pushed toward a helicopter. Blue looked back to see Robo fixed onto the orb. He laughed as he tossed it up and down. The glowing orb gently illuminated the dark surroundings.

"So little, but destined to do such big things." He tossed the glowing orb high into the air again.

It didn't come down. All Robo saw was a flash of gray flying past him, the orb disappearing with it.

"Raven," Robo growled.

Raven used his right paw to carefully push the crystal into the soft, muddy ground so it couldn't be seen. Everything became quiet except for the sound of Raven's breathing.

"Raven? Is that you, old friend?"

"Give me Blue," Raven snarled.

Although he didn't show it, Robo felt his heart torn to shreds. Like so many others, Raven was just worried about Blue. Robo stood there for a moment, helpless in his emotion.

"Give me Blue or the orb gets destroyed," Raven barked again.

Robo jumped when a twig snap, thinking it was the cracking sound of the orb.

"Okay, okay, surely we can work something out," Robo said. "Raven, join me. Let's rule together."

Raven put more weight on the ball, and it started to crack.

"Fine!" Robo snarled, and turned toward the guards. "Let her go."

The guards shoved Blue toward Raven, who quickly stepped in front of her, growling.

"Now give me the orb," Robo commanded.

Raven pulled the orb from the mud and stepped forward.

Blue, with horror in her eyes, cried out to Raven, "Don't give it to him, let him kill me."

Raven stared at Blue, his eyebrow raised. Even Blue was surprised at what she had said. Ignoring her, Raven slowly tossed the orb to Robo.

Robo grabbed it with a crazed smile.

"Perfect" he said, as he walked away. "Now, kill them both."

Instead of retreating, Blue sprang directly towards Robo, catching the robot dogs off guard. Almost instantly, Blue heard Raven's screams behind her as the guards set upon him. She didn't dare turn around. Instead, she rammed into Robo, sending him plunging into the swampy water with a splash. Blue leapt in after him, hoping to drown him. Surely his metal parts would help make him sink. No luck. Robo's robotic claws clamped onto the swamp trees, and he pulled himself back out. He turned back around to face the now-drenched Blue.

"You're a coward," she howled at him. "You let those *things* kill your best friend—didn't you?" She couldn't see through the tears in her eyes. Robo rushed forward, grabbing her by the neck and throwing her against a swamp tree.

Blue lay still.

Bitterly, Robo watched briefly to see if she was breathing. *What a waste,* he thought. *Two who could have been by my side.* He shook his head and carefully tucked the orb into its pouch around his neck. Almost immediately, he was distracted by his injured army anxious to leave the swamp—and the crocodiles behind.

"We're done here," Robo said to his dogs. "Time to take what is ours!"

The robot dogs howled and reboarded the helicopters.

As the helicopters whirled out of the swamp, Blue slowly opened her eyes. Her vision was blurry, and every part of her body ached. Clearly, Robo thought she was dead.

She remembered Raven. Slowly, she crawled over to his body, torn by the robot guards. His eyes were clouded—no more past, no more future. Just death. There were no sounds except for the frogs, the crickets, and Blue's muffled grief, as she buried her head in his bloody fur.

CHAPTER 27

ROBO FELT A WAVE OF PAIN grip his throat. It had been a long time since he had cared about any one.

They had just returned to the mountain compound, and although his army was happy—they had scattered the swamp pack, captured the orb, and killed Blue—strangely, he found he couldn't enjoy the victory.

Robo had hoped that Raven would join him. Instead, his former best friend was dead.

The news back home also wasn't great.

Unknown continued to read the reports of Robo's deputies. "We're still having problems with the armies in Europe," she said. "Many of the dogs are refusing to fight, and we're seeing more join the resistance."

Robo was tired and irritated; he closed his eyes. "I don't care about the armies right now. I don't care about anyone right now."

Unknown lowered her head and looked away. Robo caught her disdain.

"You don't matter to me," he said with a sneer. "What can you do about that?"

Unknown met his stare for the first time.

"You don't matter to me either," she said with equal intensity. "You don't matter to any of us. We're just scared of you. You used to be strong; you used to be compassionate—or at least *seemed* compassionate. I know something is not right with you." Unknown then snarled, "You don't think anyone knows your little secrets? Well, I do. I'm done with you. Kill me, torture me, I don't care. I know what a fake you really are."

Robo leapt forward, enraged, crushing her under him. But staring into her eyes, the eyes he once loved, he regained his composure.

"Unknown, let me be perfectly clear about this. I don't care what you think of me. But you *will* help me succeed. Or you will not be the only one who suffers."

He stepped to the side. Unknown jumped back up, spun around, and walked out.

Robo took out the glowing orb, fascinated by its crackling light.

Love is greatly overrated. Power is far better, he thought. *Now I have fate on my side, and things are about to change.*

CHAPTER 28

SCREENS WENT BLACK all around the world: laptops, cell phones, televisions. Radios went silent. Everyone was suddenly jarred from their mindless electronic amusements. Then the world heard the voice for the first time: deep, calm, and deadly. A huge Great Dane filled all the screens of the 21st century, his robotic eye staring directly into the camera.

"You are going to pay," he said in crisp English. "You are all going to pay for what you have done to us. You have tortured us, abandoned us, eaten us, and neglected us….and we have reached a conclusion.

"There are not too many dogs," Robo said with a snarl. "There are too many of you."

And then Robo started his first live stream to the world, recorded in the backwoods of America.

❧

Plywood surrounded the dirt pit; the walls were stained with blood. A few men were inside a trailer, but most people leaned over the walls, holding cash and screaming at each other. Growling dogs strained against their short, tight leather leashes, their owners cuffing them when they barked too much.

Pork Chop was used to this. He had such contempt for these people. They were so stupid, some with gold chains, oversized T-shirts, missing teeth, and beards. Others were in sleeveless undershirts, decked out with tattoos: women in bikinis, snakes, stars, devil wings, or some Chinese character they couldn't even read.

The Bull Terrier looked down at his paw, taking courage from the symbol burned into his pad, barely visible behind the dirt and blood. An air horn blew, and he was shoved out into the dirt, along with a scarred Pit Bull. They circled each other with deadly intent.

Both knew tonight would be different. There would be no more ruthless killing among dogs here. They had a plan. The smaller dogs had hidden the guns, and the strays had carefully unlocked the cages.

The two dogs circled each other, dodging beer bottles hurled at them when the crowd got impatient. Then they felt it—a loud rumble shook the ground.

"That's our cue," Pork Chop growled at the Pit Bull.

Immediately, they turned on their owners. Pork Chop bit down on his owner's arm; the Pit Bull clamped down on his owner's ankle. The owners started to kick and slap them, but both dogs didn't let go. Other dogs charged the audience. Some voices screamed, "Get your guns!"

In confusion, the men yelled, "Where are they? Where the hell are the guns?' They tried to fend off the snapping teeth surrounding them.

Most of the crowd ran toward the exit, but were attacked by a team of big breeds waiting for them.

Pork Chop pinned his owner to the ground, steam rising from his nostrils, his eyes bloodshot. "How could you do this to me?" he screamed. "I could kill you right now, but I have more honor than you."

The owner lay still, trying to comprehend that his dog was talking.

Pork Chop yelled, "Cowards!" to the wounded men, and joined the other dogs as they ran toward freedom.

The live feed showed the mayhem of the dog-fighting pit, with close-ups of the injured or dead gamblers and owners. The screen went black, although Robo's voice could still be heard: "We are not done," he snarled.

Within 24 hours, the humans had downloaded and shared his video. Many news programs questioned its authenticity, instead focusing on the scourge of dog fighting. As usual, they completely misread the danger they were in.

Meanwhile, Robo polished his shiny front paw, and leaned forward toward the control panel. The orb glowed, rotating slowly in its case, energy pulsing through the compound's weapons system. Robo typed in the coordinates: First, 51.5074° N, 0.1278° W. Second: 35.6895° N, 139.6917° E

❧

Robo's armies in London howled with happiness when they saw Tower Bridge collapse into the River Thames. While people reeled from the destruction, the dogs took over the streets, buildings, cars, and shops, stealing meat, stalling traffic, and snarling and snapping at all they encountered. Those who resisted paid dearly. All the while, Robo livestreamed, telling the humans that they were witnessing a new beginning: The Dawn of the Dog.

Robot armies herded humans together, imprisoning them in cages at shelters, which had been used to house strays.

Other divisions stormed through the countryside, freeing those trapped in dismal puppy mills. Everywhere they went, dogs, coyotes, and wolves created fear in humans' eyes.

Killer and his crew particularly enjoyed the chaos. His boat had been docked in the harbor for weeks as they worked non-stop on Robo's plans. Standing on the banks of the Thames, he and his soldiers sang a children's nursery rhyme as they gulped down ale from wood barrels knocked open in the street.

"All together now," Killer said, swaying slightly, and looking back at his troops. With barks and howls, they sang off-key:

London Bridge is falling down, falling down, falling down
London Bridge is falling down, my fair lady!

Killer turned and winked at a finely groomed white poodle that walked by, draped in her former owner's diamond necklaces.

Robo laughed at the mirth and mayhem. The uprising was going well. He switched monitors over to the second target: Tokyo.

The Tokyo Skytree, the tallest tower in Japan, was in ruins. Huge pieces of concrete and glass littered the streets. Young girls in their school uniforms ran screaming from their small dogs, now vicious and free of their rhinestone leashes and silly anime costumes. Thin street dogs, their ribs visible, ran boldly into sushi restaurants, leaping up on the bars, fighting over raw salmon and shrimp.

The walkways of the Imperial Palace were strewn with cherry blossom branches and abandoned weapons. Sabu stood proudly in the rubble with a strong line of Akitas.

"This is now yours," Sabu said with a flourish of his paw, presenting the palace to Robo.

"Well done, Sabu," Robo said. "Take control of the city, and then come back home."

Sabu and his troops snapped to attention. "Yes, sir."

Robo continued to watch as his forces reported victories in Rome, Beijing, and Moscow. He even joined a virtual toast of vodka-and-broth with a platoon of Russian wolfhounds on Red Square.

CHAPTER 29

"SIR?"

Robo perked his ears, and sighed when he saw it was only Savage bringing in his evening meal. He didn't want to talk to Savage right now. His future was the world, with dogs like Sabu. Savage was from his past, where his dreams were tied to nothing more than the well being of one small pack. In fact, he didn't want Savage around here anymore. With the robot dogs fully in place, Blue now dead, and the orb in his possession, there was no reason to share his power with his Beta. There was no reason for him to share his power with anyone.

Robo smiled broadly.

"Savage, we haven't talked in such a long while," he said smoothly. "I've just been so busy. Do you have any interest in taking a short walk? I need to stretch what muscles I have left."

Savage was taken aback by the sudden friendliness, but was happy that Robo had noticed him again.

"Sure!" he said, wagging his tail.

The two walked down the hallway. For Savage, this was a chance to renew an old friendship; for Robo, it was a chance for a new, solitary future.

❦

Clover pattered down the hallway, tongue lolling out of his mouth, as usual. The dogs ignored his presence since, even

179

though he looked like he could be a killer, everyone knew now that it was just a front. Clover was always in a good mood, friendly, helpful, and, in many ways, too likeable. He always just wanted everyone to get along.

Clover had found a place in the compound, and even with Robo. Despite his never-ending responsibilities, Robo would frequently summon Clover to join him for dinner. There was something about this affable dog that allowed Robo to relax and laugh. He amused him.

Now, Clover walked down the hallway to talk to Robo about the videos streaming around the world. The dogs had talked about it in hushed tones, excited about the coming war. With the orb, all the dogs in the mountain fortress knew they were now unstoppable. After months of defeat and challenges, the first video of their brothers taking over the fighting pits empowered the troops. The videos that followed were even more impressive. Robo was winning across the globe through sheer might.

Clover still wasn't sure this was the right approach. He thought if he talked to Robo, his concerns would be answered. He knocked on the door of Robo's den, and it slowly opened. Robo was nowhere to be seen.

The room was dimly lit to reduce the strain on Robo's electronic eye. Clover stepped into the room, scanning quickly. Like the control room, it was also filled with monitors, many running constant streams of data he didn't fully understand. Clover continued to walk among the monitors, low desks, and Robo's bed, his big tail swishing back and forth. He accidently knocked several papers off the desk and a photo with burned edges and a faint image—a Great Dane puppy and a girl. Clover stared at it. Getting nervous, he quickly put the photo back into place. He was ready to leave when he felt a sudden urge to see his home. It would only take a second; just a quick GPS search for his Wolfie.

He regretted it. Clover was taken aback by the grainy security image showing his former family. Wolfie seemed so sad. Clover looked closer. His father was also there. They were trapped in a small cell with a dirt floor. His dad looked exhausted and grim as he paced the cell. Wolfie looked worried and thin.

"Clover?"

Quickly, Clover switched screens, and swung around. He saw Unknown at the door.

"What are you doing?" she asked sweetly, looking around the room.

"Um, I just wanted to drop a few things off for Robo, but I tripped and just made a big mess," Clover said, using his natural clumsiness to his advantage.

"Robo and Savage have taken a walk, so I think we have time to get this back to ship-shape." She paused. "I don't really know when they're going to get back," her voice trailed off.

She narrowed her eyes at Clover again.

"Clover, are you okay?"

Clover quickly nodded, and started picking up the scattered papers. As he stacked them neatly, he used some to shield his quick close of the security screen. She wasn't paying attention any way, picking up cans, batteries, and cords. Finally, he pushed past her, trying not to show his tears.

"Yep, I'm totally fine. Don't worry about me," he said cheerily.

A new, cunning dog emerged from Robo's den, one that would use his 'niceness' to his advantage. Unknown, who had always liked sweet Clover, watched him go, before firmly closing Robo's door behind them.

⁂

Savage was getting worried about leaving the troops alone for so long without their Alpha or Beta.

"Hey, Robo, we probably should head back, yes?" he asked.

"Not quite yet," Robo said calmly. "We need to check on the humans."

Savage frowned, but didn't complain. Robo walked deeper into the compound, and started to sniff for the small cave that housed the humans.

Robo had been worried about how to keep the humans from creating more of the serum. Cynically, he discovered they were the least of his problems. If you pay them enough or promise them fame, humans would happily betray their own species.

Amazing, he thought.

Dogs, on the other hand, were much more difficult. Especially dogs like Savage. Robo didn't want or need him anymore, but Savage was so loyal, such a good leader, that even Robo couldn't kill him. He had devised a different plan.

"Savage," he said. "I want you to see this new lab we're building. We've brought in a new team of hackers to continue breaking into banking security systems. We need more money and more recruits."

Savage nodded in agreement.

Robo stepped aside. "Go ahead, check it out. I think you're

going to be amazed with what I've built."

Savage, adjusting to the dim light, stepped inside and walked carefully across the floor.

"Robo, there's really nothing here to see—"

The steel door slammed shut. Robo breathed deeply, relieved. It took a moment for Savage to realize what had happened. He started lunging at the door.

"Robo, what are you doing?" he screamed and barked. "Robo, why are you doing this?" He crumpled against the door. "I have always tried to protect you. You were like a father to me."

Robo stood quietly against the other side.

Savage, after a while, also grew quiet. "I loved you," he whispered.

Robo heard it and winced.

Love is greatly overrated, he repeated to himself as he walked away. *Power is better.*

It has to be.

CHAPTER 30

HIDING UNDER A TARP used to cover dirt and garden tools, Blue leaned close to the truck's cab window to catch the news reports on the radio about Robo's murderous worldwide march. Her fur was dirty, and her wounds painful. But that didn't slow her down. Blue was headed straight toward's Robo's compound, where Max needed her. Too many dogs were counting on her to stop the bloodshed.

Suddenly, the truck braked and swerved to avoid a group of stray dogs howling in celebration. The tailgate flew open, and Blue was thrown out the back of the truck as it accelerated again, a bale of hay breaking her fall on the pavement. She quickly got up, but her ride kept going.

"Great," she sighed.

Blue climbed to her feet and started to run next to the road. For days, she kept up the pace, only stopping for rest and water, until she was back in the pine forests of Jasper, Georgia, the mountain crest before her.

It was time to find Robo's fortified lair. In one of their many conversations, Copper had drawn her a map in the dirt in case they were separated. But her memory was failing her on the exact location.

Blue was exhausted. She was about to give up for the day, but suddenly caught a strong scent, which pushed her forward. Suddenly, it was swept away by the wind. Losing hope, she thought: *It was probably just coyotes moving through.* Her muscles ached, and her wounds were tearing open from excessive movement. She finally nestled into a pine bed, her eyes heavy, and curled up into a ball. She expected to fall asleep quickly, but her mind wouldn't let her. Instead, Blue hauled herself back up, and started pacing around the base of a mountain. *Come on Blue, you can figure this out.* As she slowly climbed through its trails, she cocked her head toward a large pile of rocks.

"Isn't that strange?" Blue whispered to herself.

Just then, she spotted paw prints in the dirt leading straight into the rocks. Blue stepped forward, and started to pull rocks off the pile, letting them roll down the hill behind her. When she uncovered the edge of a huge door, she took a step back. Emblazoned in the steel was an image of a dog encircled with a gear—Robo's symbol.

"This is it, this is Robo's base," Blue murmured. "I've got to think this through. I can't just go in there without a plan and expect to defeat Robo."

With moon rising above her, Blue took a break to sleep, hiding in a thicket of pine trees near the entrance.

The next morning, she heard the sound of small rocks tumbling by. Peeking out, she saw a large Saint Bernard bounding down the mountain, followed by about a dozen smaller dogs, all coming from the hidden door.

No way am I fighting that thing, she thought, noticing his broad shoulders, huge chest, and powerful legs. As he got closer, though, she could sense fear.

The Saint Bernard looked back toward the exit and nodded. He was clearly the leader of this little group; the other dogs circled around him in support. Blue kept herself hidden. These were clearly Robo's dogs, but they appeared to be nervous.

"If Robo finds out about this, he will have our heads!" the smallest of the dogs quivered. He kept close to the Saint Bernard.

"We won't get caught, trust me," the Saint Bernard said gently. Yet he didn't seem to believe his own words.

At that moment, he looked up—directly into Blue's eyes. *Not good,* she thought. She prepared to defend herself.

Suddenly, the Saint Bernard stood at attention with his crew. He saluted nervously in Blue's direction. "Lieutenant Clover, at your service, ma'am."

Blue was shocked, and didn't know how to respond. They were in no way threatening her, so she stepped away from her hiding place. "I am Blue, and ..."

Clover cut her off. "*The* Blue? Blue of the prophecy? We thought you were dead."

Blue shifted nervously. "Please state your business."

"We're leaving to join the resistance."

Blue didn't believe him for a moment.

Clover could tell, so he continued. "I came to this place to learn how to protect my family, whom I love and who love me. I have learned that things are not what I thought, and my family is in trouble. I have to help them."

Blue stared at him. There was no indication that he was lying. The dogs behind him trembled as he confessed to treason.

"I have learned the ways of Robo's army, and more importantly, the ways of Robo himself." He paused, letting Blue absorb what he just said. "I have used my position to learn about this complex—its strengths, and its weaknesses. Robo promised us—promised me—to make dogs and humans equal partners. But everything he has said is a lie. He is not a leader. He is a tyrant.

"We were on our way to meet up with SAD. We hear they now have a powerful resistance, and since we are familiar with the inner workings of RAD, we thought we might be useful."

Blue was taken aback. She hadn't considered that the dogs under Robo's leadership might have doubts, especially in light of their recent victories. She nodded; she understood the significance of what Clover was offering.

"I'm sure you are right. Let's go together, and we can plan the next steps."

Clover nodded to his troops, who fell in behind him as Blue led them down the mountain. When they turned around the last bend of a long-forgotten trail, Blue saw Jenny. Overjoyed, she ran up to Jenny, their tails both wagging. "How did you know to come here?" Blue asked.

"Well," Jenny said. "We cleaned out the base on the beach, and after reading files, we learned about the headquarters here. And…I brought friends."

Over the pine ridge, Blue saw thousands of dogs carefully approaching the base of the mountain, using the shrubs and trees as cover. Many were battle-scarred, but there were some yearlings and puppies, including the now-healed, half-robot Rover.

"Blue, I think you remember Rex," said Jenny, as a coyote scrambled up the mountain.

Blue was so relieved to see Rex. Rex meant SAD—and SAD meant they weren't on their own.

"Fuzzy Wuzzy! Good to see you!" he yipped. Looking around, he asked, "Where is Copper?" Blue looked down, Rex raised an eyebrow. "Blue?"

Blue looked up at him, took a deep breath, and sighed, "Copper...Copper has moved on."

Rex took a step back and went silent.

"Jenny, Rex, we have lost too many good dogs. We must put an end to the fighting. Today, a group of courageous young officers, formerly of Robo's army, has offered to help us."

Jenny narrowed her eyes. "I know—they contacted SAD. I don't totally trust them."

Rex cocked his head, "I agree. SAD doesn't always make the best decisions when it comes to trust."

"Well, I trust these dogs," Blue said. "There's something about their leader. He misses his family a lot. And recently, I've learned what that's like."

"Fine," Jenny said. "We will assign one officer from his group to each pack. They will get us into the mountain and act as our guides. Of course, if they turn on us, we will kill them without hesitation."

Blue nodded her head in agreement, before Jenny and Rex barked orders to assemble the troops. Blue felt tension lift from her chest. For once, someone had listened to her.

Jenny and Rex climbed the ledge, with Blue behind them. They parted, allowing Blue to walk between them, ascending to the highest point of the ridge, looking out over the huge gathering of dogs. She howled, the sound echoing across the mountain. The dogs were stunned. They had heard about Blue: the Chosen One with powers equal to Robo's. Here she was! Alive! Ready to fight!

She spoke firmly, her aqua eyes glowing with passion. "Brothers and sisters, rejoice! Good always rises up. I am here to join you, to lead you—if you'll have me—in a battle to restore balance and save the dogs and humans we love." She paused. "I come here for my pups, Max and Destiny. Who do you come for? Who are you fighting to save?

"We will not let our species fall into the trap of revenge. We will fight for love, not hate. We will not let a dictator choose which humans we will love, and which ones we will not. We will choose our own destinies, without the harsh hand of technology or fear of evil. Let us restore honor, and take our rightful place as protectors of this world, not destroyers."

The dogs barked in unison. The leaders quieted the crowds and told them to take position.

Blue turned to Clover. "Now, show us how get us in," she ordered.

"Yes, ma'am. Follow me."

He led a small patrol, which included Blue, Jenny, Ash, Rex, and Rover. Soon after pushing several rocks aside, they saw the steel door.

Clover showed Blue the imprint of the gear on his paw. "My security clearance no longer works," Clover said, apologetically. "I'm sure they killed it as soon as I showed up missing." Blue looked at the patrol and realized she had a solution. She needed another member of Robo's army—someone less important who would still be in the system, undetected and unnoticed.

"Rover," she called. "Step forward."

Nervously, the puppy came forward with Ash.

"Rover, this is your moment. You are making a difference,"

Blue said gently, as she took his front paw and put it on the scanner.

The monitor scanned his imprint, clicked green, and the door opened.

"Good dog," Jenny said proudly.

Ash proudly licked Rover on his nose. "My son."

PART 4

And tyranny and history do not own the future. She, separated
from the he, will dig, demand and restore
The chance for a new balance.

CHAPTER 31

THE NEXT DAY, the SAD army approached the mountains, accompanied by Clover's officers. The resistance slipped quietly through the hallways. The water dogs slid through sewer tunnel openings, hiding in the shadows and waiting for Blue's signal.

"Remember, we don't kill civilians," Blue said to the troops. "our goals are for them to surrender, and to retrieve the orb." She took a deep breath and howled, "Attack!"

Dogs were everywhere, through the halls, in the tunnels, running across the auditorium, setting upon Robo's forces.

Blue walked through the door, her heart pounding as adrenaline shook her feet. Her eyes grew sharp. She knew that her only mission—her destiny—was to find Robo.

She didn't have to search for long. Robo sat there, a crazed smile on his face as he watched his armies attack the SAD troops. He turned and stared at her in disbelief.

"Why won't you just die?" he snarled. He quickly regained his composure.

"Oh Blue, missing something?"

He held up the orb.

"Come and get it!" he yelled, as he turned and leapt over the fighting dogs and disappeared into the tunnels.

Blue's ears lowered as she realized that the auditorium was complete chaos, packed with injured and slain dogs. Jenny limped toward her.

"Look around, Blue," Jenny rasped. "We are taking casualties, but his armies are taking more."

Blue followed her gaze, looking out at a sea of titanium dogs. Looking closer, she noticed that many had battle wounds, but also infected cuts, torn skin, and malnourished bodies.

"Get as many as possible to surrender as we originally planned," Blue said to Jenny. "Kill them if you must—they could still be dangerous—but try to take prisoners insteaad."

Jenny nodded and headed back into battle, snarling and nipping as titanium claws tried to cut her.

Blue saw an opening, sprinted through the auditorium, and slid into the hallway to the right of the control room, hoping to find a back entrance. It was dimly lit, but she was able to pick up a familiar scent. There was a cage to the right of her. Blue quickly ran forward to unlock the bars.

"Max! Oh Max!" she cried, as the golden lab—no longer a puppy—cowered in fear. He was starving, with matted fur, and dark circles under his eyes.

"Blue?" he asked hesitantly. "BLUE!" Max limped foward, bursting into tears.

Blue whimpered when he fell into her fur, her eyes burned with tears.

"Yes, honey, it's really me," Blue whispered in his ear, her voice tender. Never had she been so happy to see anyone in her life.

"You came back for me?" Max asked haltingly, his tears making her fur damp.

"Of course," she said. "I will always come back for you. Always."

Max moved away from her, back into his cage. "I'll be safe

for now," he said. "Nobody cares about me to bother me. But you must go stop Robo, Blue."

"Be careful, Max," Blue said. Max joyfully barked, and for the first time in months, slowly wagged his tail.

CHAPTER 32

BLUE WAS FRUSTRATED. The first hallway had provided the happy discovery of Max, but brought her no closer to finding Robo. She quickly headed back to the main hall, toward Robo's control room. A mesmerizing scene in the auditorium caused her to slow down.

The robot dogs no longer outnumbered SAD. Now there were hundreds of dogs: Border Collies, Huskies, German Shepherds, Pit Bulls, even Scottish Terriers and Chihuahuas, biting and snapping at the robot dogs, telling them to surrender.

Rex had a slash across his cheek. He briefly barked at her, but instead was forced to defend himself. "This is for you, Copper," he barked.

Blue headed down the tunnel to the left, still looking for a back entrance. It was even darker than the others. Before long, she sensed a dog behind her. With ears down and fur up, she recognized the smell, and then the voice.

"I remember the first time Robo and I met," Splat said, inching toward Blue. "I can still feel his paw on my snout. I can still see my pack leader—dead because of him." Splat's voice had a strange electronic echo to it. "My pack leader was a fool."

He slowly moved toward her side and revealed his face. Like Robo, metal implants covered his face.

Blue took a step back. "Splat? What happened to you?"

Splat smiled, blood staining his teeth. "I was upgraded from the pathetic dog I was." He paused. "Oh Blue, you have so much potential. Join us, and you will have power you can only dream of. We will build a brand new world where you never have to worry about hunger, disease, or abuse. Where we are the masters of all."

Blue snarled, "Never!"

Splat narrowed his eyes. "So be it."

He sprang toward her, raking his metal claws down her chest. She jumped back in pain, and then leaped above him, catching his paw in her teeth. He gave a yelp of pain. Splat charged her again, this time pushing her against the wall, biting deep into her neck. Blue used the wall as a brace, and then raked his stomach with her back legs. He howled with pain.

"You're no different from any other dog!"

Blue laughed. "No Splat. I'm very different from every other dog. I am the Chosen One."

She then bit his robotic eye and yanked back, puling as hard as she could. Suddenly, she hit the opposite wall, his robotic eye still in her mouth. Splat howled as electric wires and green fluid spewed from his eye socket. He collapsed, growling at Blue.

Blue gasped.

With his electronic eye gone, Splat's rage seemed to have faded from him. Passing in and out of consciousness, he looked up at her with a dazed squint and asked, "Where am I?" His natural eye was full of sorrow, and he was bleeding from several wounds. Finally, he laid his head down between his paws. With his head turned, he looked like the dog she used to know.

Blue gently whispered, "I'm sorry, Splat." And she was.

Behind her, a female's voice broke the silence. "Oh Splat!"

Blue yelled, "Stay back, cat!"

Unknown didn't listen, pushing past Blue with eyes full of tears.

"Oh Splat! Why did you agree to this?" Unknown whispered, lying beside him.

Blue hadn't realized how much Unknown cared for him. Unknown stayed by his side, using her paws to wipe away his tears, frantically trying to lick his wounds.

Splat turned toward Unknown, and nuzzled with her. "I'm not dead yet," he said in a small, raspy voice.

"What?" Unknown asked shakily.

"Unknown, this is our chance. If you can just help me a little bit, we can leave all of this. Leave Robo, and start over, just you and me."

Unknown's grief turned into cautious happiness.

"Splat, you're right. This was never our battle to begin with," she murmured.

Splat hauled himself to a sitting position, and looked at Blue apologetically.

Blue tried to speak but someone else cut her off.

"You!" Duncan yelled at Unknown, running toward her with anger. "Running away again!

"You're weak. You've always been weak. Just look at all the pain you have caused."

Unknown stared down at her paws. Splat stepped in between her and Duncan.

Duncan glared at Splat, then at Blue. "This stupid excuse for a mother left me on my own, when I needed her the most."

Unknown stared at Duncan. "I'm so sorry I wasn't there for

you. I was scared of Robo. Terrified of him. "

Duncan snorted. "You think fear ever stopped me? No, and I'm doing just fine on my own!"

Suddenly another dog emerged behind him. Blue hadn't realized Destiny was standing with Duncan, her black fur blending her into the dimly lit hall.

"Duncan, there are limits to what any dog can endure," Destiny said quietly. "You know more than most what fear can do."

Unknown stood up and looked at Duncan. "Please, son. I'm sorry for all the ways that I have failed you. I was afraid that if I did not go with Robo, he would kill you. And that would have killed me.

"I hope, someday you can forgive me," she said. "But right now, can you find it in your heart to let me start over—with Splat? He has been my partner for years, and loves me as much as I suspect this young Destiny loves you"

Splat stumbled to his feet and rose to his full height. His eye socket was no longer bleeding.

"Both of us will be slaughtered by Robo without a second thought," he told Duncan. "Your mother doesn't deserve that."

Duncan looked confused, but relaxed when Destiny slipped under his chin, looking up at him lovingly.

"Duncan, let them go," Destiny said. "We have all done things we regret. Let your mother have a second chance. For her and for you."

Duncan lovingly looked into Destiny's eyes and sighed. "I'm only doing this for Destiny's sake. Get out of here, find a safe place, and never come back."

Unknown limped to Duncan and nuzzled his ear. "Thank you. Thank you so much, Duncan," she said. "I will make things right. I promise."

Duncan stood stiff, but slowly accepted her embrace. "Go. Now."

Destiny stepped forward to briefly nuzzle Unknown and Splat before they ran out of the room, seeking a secret passage that would free them from the compound forever.

Duncan turned to Destiny. "You owe me."

Destiny rolled her eyes. "Yeah, right."

Blue couldn't absorb all that she had just witnessed. Unknown and Splat were happily headed to freedom from Robo. Her Destiny was with a worthy partner, who obviously loved her. A happy moment in the middle of hell.

Destiny said firmly to Blue. "You have a mission to complete. We'll hold off his armies as long as we can," she said, with a slow grin. "Now, you go save the world."

Duncan nodded to her. "Good luck, you're going to need it."

They both turned around and sprinted back to the auditorium.

Blue sat there for a moment, in the strange silence of the hall. Slowly, she looked around—it had to be here, somewhere. She noticed the small lever. This was it. Pushing it down, she heard a large clanging sound followed by silence. As Blue walked toward the great steel door, she knew she could never turn away from her fate. She pushed the now unlocked door open, and walked in.

CHAPTER 33

OKAY, BLUE. THIS IS IT.

She saw Robo's silhouette illuminated by the glow of monitors. Blue narrowed her eyes. Images flashed through her mind: Destiny, Max, Copper, Duncan, and Raven. She snarled, causing Robo to whip around, clearly in shock.

"How on earth did you—?"

Blue smirked. "I'm a hard dog to kill—remember?"

Robo narrowed his eyes. "Well, I guess I'll have to make sure the job gets done this time."

"Look, Robo. For the last time, you don't have to do this," she said. "Just stop. You still have time to change."

Robo curled his lips. "And do what? Let humans rule? Put up with more abuse, more death, and more destruction?"

Blue shook her head. "Have you even looked at what you're doing, Robo?" she said. "You're causing death, you're causing abuse. At the rate you're going, you'll destroy the world itself. You've lost your way, Robo. You're better than this."

Robo's eyes widened in fury. "You think you know what's going on, you naïve dog? You haven't even scratched the surface!"

"Maybe," she said slowly, "but I do know one thing." She looked him directly in the eye. "Would Becca want this?"

Robo took a step back, avoiding her gaze. "I don't know what you're talking about, city mutt."

Blue had reached into her leather bag, pulling out Becca's

drawing. "I know you loved her with all your heart. Would she really want all this death and destruction? Do you even know if she's still alive?"

Blue slid the paper toward Robo, his eye wide with sorrow as he stared down at it.

"You still have the power to stop this. Let's find another way—for both the SAD and the RAD armies." Blue said in a whisper.

Robo looked at Blue, his eye wet. "I've gone too far, Blue." Then he smiled, tears still streaming down his face. "And now, so have you!"

He sprang at Blue, his jaws snapping. Robo grabbed Blue by the scruff and flung her, causing her to slide against the main control panel and fall to the floor. Before she could try to get up, Robo gripped her again, and threw her hard against the wall. She lay there motionless.

Robo walked toward her. "So weak. It's amazing how you've managed to survive this long."

Blue slowly got up. She felt her heart pounding. She sprang at him, clawing his ears. He yelped, but quickly bit her paw, crushing it. She howled in pain and used her other paw to kick him in the jaw as he sprang away. Blue followed him, catching his front metal leg. Her powers were as strong as his, and she felt the titanium leg bend and fail. He yelped once again, and tore at her ear. She quickly scrambled up, staring at him. His leg was twisted and crushed, bright green liquid mixing with blood onto the cold gray floor. He unclenched his teeth, and spat out some of her ear.

Blue felt blood stream down her face, but it didn't stop her.

She jumped at him once more. He lowered his head, ready for the impact. This time, she was able to pin him against the floor. He sneered at her.

"Bad move, Blue."

He used his powerful legs to kick her far into the air, smashing through the control room's narrow windows.

She heard the sound of glass breaking as she landed in the mud outside. Pouring rain drenched her fur in seconds. She slowly, painfully rose and looked around.

Her vision was blurry, but she saw…humans? Wearing camouflage and carrying rifles, they had detected the battle and found Robo's hideaway. Helicopters and drones hovered above the mountain.

Suddenly she heard the sound of more breaking glass. Looking up, she saw Robo standing over her. He snarled once, before shoving her toward a rock. Her vision was dimly red and blurred even more. She wobbled around, her mouth gaping— everything seemed unrecognizable. Through the haze, she recognized Robo's glowing red eye. Blue lunged toward him, and they battled back toward the compound. Further they climbed, until they wrestled on a rock ledge and tumbled back through a window, landing on the hard concrete floor.

Robo had broken her fall. "Get off of me," he howled, raking his claws down her stomach. He kicked her again onto the floor, leaving a smear of blood.

She didn't get back up. *This is it*, she thought. *I'm not strong enough.*

Still, her mind raced for options, and found none. She tried to get up to no avail.

Robo howled in triumph. "You're going to die, Blue. You've irritated me for too long."

Robo limped toward her, and put his broken robotic paw on her throat, its sharp claws digging in. Blue wheezed for breath, her eyes blood-shot. She felt her flesh give in to the metal claws, and red flooded her vision. She saw images of her mother, and all the friends she had made during her journey. She was going to fail them all.

No, I refuse. I will not fail. Blue's eyes snapped open, and she struck Robo right in the robotic eye with her good paw. He jumped away, turning his back toward her. Blue shakily rose to her feet. Looking down at her neck, she could see the deep cut across her chest.

Then she noticed her necklace. Through everything, the necklace and leather pouch had stayed with her. She stared at Robo, who still had his back turned from her. She quickly removed the necklace, and looped it around Robo's neck. Yanking it hard with her teeth, she tried to choke him.

"Die!" Robo hissed, as he pulled, giving a hard yank back, which snapped the necklace and sent the pendant of the Husky across the floor.

Robo gasped for breath. Liquid streamed from his robotic eye, burning what was left of the fur on his face. He charged forward, and Blue quickly swerved out of the way. She doubled back, and snapped her teeth on his robotic tail. Using his weight against him, she tripped him, causing him to stumble out of the control room and onto the catwalk. The cables rattled as Robo's weight hit it.

Blue followed him onto the catwalk as Robo got up again,

and took a defensive position.

"I ALWAYS WIN!" Robo roared.

He sprang at Blue. The catwalk cables shook again; they both realized they were dangerously suspended over the pool of acid.

At the same time, the mountain rumbled—the humans were starting to attack; small bits of rock started to fall into the pit while they fought.

For one moment, everything was deadly silent. Then there was a crack as one of the catwalk's cables snapped, the entire metal platform groaning as it shifted and tipped toward the pool of acid below.

Robo slid close to the edge, and used his robotic front leg to hold himself in place. The cable had snapped on Robo's side, so Blue had an easier time staying on the platform. Blue tried to stay calm and still. Robo could not contain the rage burning in him. Howling and snarling, he accidentally gave a push of his leg and another cable on his side broke. The catwalk shifted again, sending Robo tumbling to the ledge of the acidic pit. Blue yelped in surprise, and dug her claws into the mesh to hold on as she watched Robo slide off. She sprang to the safety on the concrete floor. As she crouched there, her body trembled with the adrenaline.

With his two titanium paws, Robo had managed to hold on to the lip of the pit, hanging a couple of feet above the acid.

"Blue, I'm sorry. Please, just help me up," he said. "I will not win this. I see how pointless all of this is. Let me up so I can call the armies off. I don't want even more dogs or humans to die."

Blue thought of leaving him, but she shook her head. *Killing him like this will make me no better than he is.*

"I'll try."

"Please pull me up by the scruff," he directed. As Blue leaned forward, she saw Robo's viciousness return.

"You're such a fool," he snarled, as he tried to knock her off balance into the pit. "Now witness my superiority, you pup!"

Two metal wings deployed from his shoulders, rising above the pool.

"This is your day to meet death, not mine," he yelled, as he slowly flew toward the gaping hole where there had been windows. Escape looked easy.

Blue cowered as the complex shook again as explosives hit the side of the mountain. Both Blue and Robo were startled as a chunk of the ceiling fell, smashing into one of Robo's wings. He started to spiral, descending with the rest of the debris. Robo couldn't gain control, smashing into the crumbling walls and monitors. His good wing spun him so he landed near Blue, blocking the exit.

He wheezed as he slowly got up from the fall. He was now almost completely blind, his robotic eye broken, and his natural eye filled with blood. Some of his canine teeth were missing. A large splinter of glass was stuck in his hip. For a brief moment, Blue saw him as the old dog he was, skinny and frail, with a white nose and a broken metal tail.

Yet, he was not ready for defeat.

He stood there, mildly confused. "What happened? Becca? Anyone?" Then Robo's gaze finally landed on Blue, and all of his confusion slowly turned to anger.

"You," he said. "Always you."

He attacked.

Blue was backed up against the wall with nowhere to run. As she turned her head to prepare for Robo's impact, she noticed the spotlights from the humans' helicopters shining through the broken windows. One of the lights flashed into Blue's eyes, temporarily blinding her.

With only seconds before Robo would reach her, Blue grabbed a large shard of mirrored glass and angled it toward him, reflecting the spotlight and blinding him. Robo tried to stop running when the light hit him, but his broken leg slid under him, causing him to trip and slide into the pool of acid.

Blue crawled to the edge.

"Enough is enough, Robo," she said. "Your reign is over."

This time, there was no remorse, and no games.

Robo snarled at her, and tried to swipe her with his titanium front paw. He missed and slipped under the surface.

Blue looked away in horror.

Robo was gone without a sound.

CHAPTER 34

BLUE TURNED AROUND, feeling anything but victorious. Her ear was torn, and she had a piece of glass still stuck in her leg. She couldn't hear; her ears were ringing from the explosions and gunfire.

Blue pushed on through the steel doors and down the hall to the main battle. It was chaos. Suddenly, the robots stopped and stared at each other. Their leaders howled, "Robo is dead! Retreat!"

They leaped over the SAD dogs and broken equipment, dropping into the sewers. From there, they burst outside, nipping at the human soldiers, and running into the forest. They were quickly joined by the rest of the RAD army, an injured, fierce German Shepherd with dark eyes leading the retreat. The last robot dog to leave paused briefly to flip a switch, releasing sliding doors that closed and sealed the sewer lines from the outside. The SAD armies didn't chase them, instead breaking into cheers of celebration.

Blue stared at the fleeing dogs, her concentration only broken by Max's voice.

"Blue! Blue, you're alive!" Max yipped happily, as he limped toward her and nuzzled her.

Duncan walked toward Blue. "Is he really dead?" he asked her quietly.

"Yes, he's dead," she said, closing her eyes to block out the image.

Their happiness was short-lived. They continued to feel the explosions shaking the compound, but now there were voices of soldiers near the entrance of the complex.

"What are we going to do?" Jenny yelped.

The complex shook again with another explosion.

"Look, they're going to blow this place up," Rex said, quietly to Blue. "We have to get all these dogs outta here, or we're all going to die."

Blue nodded her head in agreement. She turned to Max, Destiny, and Duncan.

"As soon as we get out of this mountain, I want you to run to the city," Blue told them. "Do you understand me? If I don't return..." her voice drifted off. "Well, you have a responsibility to keep going—together, as a family."

They grimly lowered their heads and nodded.

"Time to get going," Blue called to them, looking for Rex.

She finally caught a glimpse of him briefly with another Husky who looked vaguely familiar.

"Let's do this, team. We haven't won this battle yet," the Husky howled through the crowd. "Everyone needs to move out. Get your pups and get going. Soldiers, prepare!"

Blue couldn't see the Husky clearly from the distance, but she picked up a faint scent. It couldn't be. Was it the smell of coffee?

Then the Husky—wearing an earphone and microphone— turned her graceful head, and gazed warmly at her.

"Mom?" Blue yelped. "Is it really you? How did you...?"

Her mom walked forward, tears in her own blue eyes, and nuzzled her. Everything around seemed to blur except her.

"How are you still alive?" Blue asked.

"I had cancer until recently," her mom said gently. "The humans at the coffee house got me help and medicine. They saved my life."

Blue stepped back. Over time, she had harbored so much anger and grief toward those at the coffee shop. "I thought they had killed you," she said sorrowfully.

"Things are not always what they seem," Diamond said. "Those you think could not possibly help end up being the ones who make the biggest difference."

Rex trotted next to Diamond.

"We have got to get this started," he said with urgency.

Blue swallowed deeply, her legs still wobbly from fatigue and injury. She narrowed her eyes, and nodded.

"Let's do this."

Diamond commanded platoons of large breed dogs to quickly push the rubble out of the hallways, while she prepared the others to storm out of the mountain. In the control room, Clover opened the steel doors guarding the main entrance of the complex, much to the surprise of the human soldiers who were slowly climbing through the mountain terrain.

Blue barked commands to both pack dogs and SAD forces. It was raining hard, a mixed blessing, giving an advantage to the nimble dogs that could handle the mud and rocks better than the humans.

"Which dog was it?" a sergeant yelled to his troops. He aimed his gun at a poodle. "Was it you?" he asked, his gun shaking. He swung it around at a German Shepherd. "Or maybe it was you." He turned around again, and then leveled the gun at Max. "No, it was you."

He slowly started squeezing the trigger, his hand still shaking. Blue sprang forward, seeing the flash of light as the gun fired. She landed right in front of Max, but felt a sharp, burning pain in her tail. She howled in pain.

Blue took a moment to absorb what had happened. She stepped toward the man. The sergeant raised his gun again.

"Why?" she yelled at him. "Why would you shoot? It's just like humans to act first and think second."

All the soldiers backed up. They had heard that the dogs could now talk to humans, but had yet to witness it firsthand.

The sergeant pointed the gun again.

"Step back, dog, or I'll kill you," he said, bracing his arm.

She stepped forward, snarling, causing the sergeant to trip backwards and land in the mud. As he prepared to aim again, Blue heard a loud snarl. She looked up to see that the humans had been completely encircled by the snow pack, led by Balta. Balta growled in his ear.

"Raise that gun again, and I'll tear your throat out."

With the tables turned, the human leaders commanded a retreat.

Balta then leaned down to Blue. "I think you're going to live," she said with a chuckle, as she checked the small bullet wound on Blue's tail.

Balta finished getting all dogs out of the mountain, working with Clover, Jenny, and SAD. They moved the rocks back in front of the entrance.

Hours later, Blue was resting, her body patched up from the battle. Balta came to see her.

"You know, we found Buddy," Balta said. "Tell me you

didn't kill him."

Blue sadly looked at Balta. "Of course not. They used him to get to me."

She shook her head—another casualty of Robo's Dawn of the Dogs.

"I'll let you rest here for a couple of moments, but it's not wise to stay in this one spot. The humans will be trying to catch as many of us as possible," Balta said.

Blue nodded. "I can travel. I just need a couple of moments."

Balta dipped her head in respect. "I'm sorry, but it's for the good of all of us."

Balta turned away, and trotted out.

Clover came in. Fur had been torn from his pelt, and he had a deep wound in his chest. Blue was still wincing in pain.

"Um, Blue?"

Blue looked up at him. "Yes?"

"I wanted to say thank you," he said. "You don't get to meet The Chosen One every day."

Then Clover shifted his feet. "I think I'm going to leave now."

Blue cocked her head. "Why?"

"I need to find my family. I'm worried about them. My Wolfie is out there, and I don't want him to get hurt anymore." Clover sighed, lifting his paw to show Robo's symbol. "I already will have to live with this forever."

Blue nodded. "You go find your family," she said, then giving him the highest compliment she could: "You are a good dog." She licked Clover's shoulder, "Good luck."

Clover nodded before turning away and heading toward the coast and a boat to return home.

CHAPTER 35

BLUE WALKED DOWN the familiar old alley, a large rat in her jaws. She was still limping badly, but the rat hadn't had a chance.

Blue turned toward her old den, watching Destiny licking her sleek fur, and Max scratching behind his ears. They jumped in surprise when she sat down in front of them, dropping the rat.

Max wrinkled his nose and spat, "How do you eat this stuff?"

Blue turned around, acting insulted, and put her paw on his chest.

"If you were an alley dog, you would understand."

"Well, luckily," he said, "I'm not alley dog. I'm a city dog."

Duncan then revealed he had a hot dog, which he then laid next to Destiny.

"Here you go," he said proudly, but then his stomach rumbled, and he looked longingly at the dead rat.

It had been a month since the Great Battle, as SAD referred to it. Blue still felt sore. One of her paws ended up being broken, and it was still tender.

"Look, I shouldn't even be hunting for you, lazy bones!"

Max twitched his floppy ears. "Okay Fuzzy Wuzzy!" he said with a laugh.

"Blue! Blue!"

She quickly turned and saw her mom, Diamond, running toward her. They nuzzled, her mom still breathless. Blue smelled the scent of coffee on her mom's fur, and patiently waited for her to catch her breath.

"I have a present for you," her mom said, slyly. "For you, Blue," and then playfully, pulling on Max's and Destiny's ears, "and you, and you!"

She carried a sack around her neck. She dipped her head, and the sack dropped. Leftover gluten-free sandwiches with bacon and eggs spilled out for everyone. Diamond then signaled to Blue. "Keep digging," she said, with a laugh. Blue, sticking her head fully into the sack, could not contain her own joy.

"Potatoes!" Blue yipped, unable to control herself. Immediately, she started rolling them and tossing them in the air. Destiny and Diamond joined in.

Max rolled his eyes. "Blue, you are such an alley dog."

He didn't have a chance to say more as the three other dogs leaped on him playfully, forcing him to roll on his belly.

As the dogs tumbled and tossed their toys, they were too busy to notice the handful of humans chatting around a television that had been rolled out on the sidewalk. The humans' voices tuned out the popular local channel, but Blue could not ignore the sound of the anchorman discussing the "ongoing reports of dogs attacking humans," before warning viewers that some might find "this footage disturbing."

The humans briefly stopped. "This is the good part," one muttered. On the screen, a powerful Husky barked at troops among the rubble of Robo's mountain enclave.

The anchorman said ominously, "Stay tuned to our special report tomorrow: Family pet or lethal killer?" He turned brightly to his co-anchor. "Now, Kristen, why don't you tell us more about Atlanta's Krispy Kreme charity giveaway this weekend. Viewers, do nut miss it."

Kristen and the weatherman started to fake chuckle. "You are *so* funny, Brad," she said, tossing her blonde hair.

Meanwhile, Max turned to Blue. "Okay," he finally said. "How exactly do you eat these potatoes?"

Blue and Diamond laughed.

"You don't eat them, silly," said Blue, pushing him gently. "You play with them. Like the good alley dog you should be."

Max sprang forward, tossing one in the air and catching it. He did it again, and again. He stopped when he saw his entire adoptive family was watching him in amusement.

"That's, um, surprisingly fun," he said, noticing Blue's and Diamond's amused expressions. He turned away, his eyes narrowed. "I'm not apologizing."

Blue looked at him, Destiny, Duncan, and Diamond. She was at peace. To Blue, everything seemed perfect.

But perfection never lasts.

CHAPTER 36

DOGS. Most seem nice. But some are just evil.

Everything felt numb. His eye was forced close, and he couldn't breathe.

Was he dead?

He shook his head. No. Apparently, living was his punishment.

Robo had been built to withstand a nuclear blast, so the acid was merely a setback. Much of his fur was burned away, his skin was damaged, but most of his robotic parts were still working—with the green fluid running through his body keeping him alive—if just barely.

It was so peaceful down here, so quiet. It had been a long time since he had such solitude.

Robo started to swim upward. Robo broke through the acid with huge gulps of air. He was able to crawl to the landing. Walking past the sparking wires, and the broken cables in the control room, he was hit with the smells of war: humans, burning rubble, and Blue.

"You thought this was over," Robo said, under his breath. "Clearly, you are wrong."

He turned and called to the dogs that remained, some trapped by fallen beams, others injured, and a few too disoriented to leave.

"We will rebuild," Robo barked to the dogs. Many of them

exchanged glances, or simply ignored him. A few wagged their tails, and howled with pleasure.

Robo limped back to his private quarters. Even he wondered exactly how he had survived. Only one man knew the answer: Dr. Dexter Rune. Too bad he was dead.

His natural eye looked at his reflection in a piece of broken glass. With no robotic eye, and barely any teeth, Robo looked more like a skeleton than a dog.

That wasn't important. He had averted death. He had another chance.

"Oh, Blue," he snarled. "We're not done yet. You forget I always win."

He climbed over the broken glass and concrete in the control room, back to his den, hidden by rubble and dirt. His natural eye still was recognized by the retinal scanner, and the steel door opened. Robo quietly entered the room, letting the cool darkness comfort him. As he stepped across the floor, his paw slid on a piece of paper. He looked down, only to discover it was the faded photo of him and Becca that he had kept to all these years.

He shoved it aside, sending it swooping across the room, only to fall behind a darkened monitor.

Love is pain, and he had had enough. Robo curled into his bed, now at peace, slipping into a deep sleep. He had survived another night—and he would see another dawn.

THE PROPHECY

When good twists into bad, and bad grows into good
And flesh and steel become one,
Red will rule the world,
And all with prints will suffer.
But from deep waters, one will rise
With bones buried at her feet and gems for vision,
Who will show that rage does not justify revenge,
And tyranny and history do not own the future.
She, separated from the he, will dig, demand and restore
The chance for a new balance.

ACKNOWLEDGEMENTS

My best friends Ashley and Brooke Beaty for reading this from the very beginning, and giving me great feedback on what I did well and what I could make better. Paul Sepe, who copy-edited this book, and asked me nicely to become a better speller. Artist Elizabeth Landt, for designing awesome concepts for the cover, and listening closely to what I wanted. Emily Logan, my older "sister" and lifelong reader, for doing an intense run-through of my book, checking for logic errors and plot holes (no steaming broth!) Daphne Hopkins, my art teacher, who let me draw and work with her during recess since I was seven. Hannah Hoy, my fourth grade teacher, who put up with me writing this book during school when I should have been studying. Billy Raymer, for teaching me how to get started with animation, and is kind of funny, too. Papaw (David Lore), for keeping 7-Up in the fridge for me. The Westin Hotel at the Perimeter, in the shadow of the "King" and "Queen" in Atlanta, for fun editing nights. Balta, Buddy, and our new puppy, Zoey, (as well as Jenny, Nick, and Jack), for being our family's silly, wonderful dogs and showing me how great animals can be.

CPSIA information can be obtained
at www.ICGtesting.com
Printed in the USA
LVOW12s2241030317
526104LV00004B/4/P